"The kid's got wheels," Slingshot said approvingly as Orlando shot across the outfield. "I'll bet he really flies on grass."

Orlando raced under the ball and made a fantastic catch. Then he tried to stop running. He dug in his heels, but it didn't take. The hardened crust of snow was too slippery. He kept right on going, slip-sliding away at breakneck speed.

"Look out!" I yelled from third base. "Look out for the wall!"

The whole team held its breath.

Mr. Bones came over and stood beside me. That short-legged, long-nosed, yellow-haired fur ball liked to be petted and liked to lick faces. He did not like to see people barrel into walls. He hid his face behind my knees.

Sha-bam!

Orlando smashed into the boards like a runaway train.

KEVIN MARKEY

HARPER
An Imprint of HarperCollins Publishers

Walloper and his classmates are studying the poems
"Father Time Is Coming" by J. Patrick Lewis
(pp. 78–79) and "Watermelon" by Charles Simic
(pp. 107–108) in class.

The Super Sluggers: Wall Ball
Copyright © 2010 by Kevin Markey
All rights reserved.
Printed in the United States of America.
No part of this book may be used or reproduced in any manner whatsoever without written permission except in the case of brief quotations embodied in critical articles and reviews. For information address HarperCollins Children's Books, a division of HarperCollins Publishers, 10 East 53rd Street, New York, NY 10022.

www.harpercollinschildrens.com

Library of Congress Cataloging-in-Publication Data
Markey, Kevin.
    Wall ball / Kevin Markey. — 1st ed.
        p.   cm. — (Super sluggers)
    Summary: As the boys of the Rambletown Rounders get ready for another baseball season, spring training is taking place in the snowiest weather Rambletown has ever seen.
    ISBN 978-0-06-115223-8
    [1.   Baseball—Fiction. 2.   Snow—Fiction. 3. Schools—Fiction.] I. Title.
    PZ7.M3394546Wal 2010   2009014266
    [Fic]—dc22   CIP
                                                           AC

Typography by Larissa Lawrynenko
11 12 13 14 15   CG/CW   10 9 8 7 6 5 4 3 2 1
❖
First paperback edition, 2011

For Sarah and Nat,
a couple of champs

★ CHAPTER 1 ★

"Mr. Bones," I said, "I'm sorry to be the one to tell you this, but you look ridiculous. Absolutely ridiculous."

Mr. Bones cocked his floppy-eared head to one side and wagged his tail like a palm tree in a hurricane.

A real palm tree would have been nice. It would have meant tropical weather. As it was, we were stuck in the middle of the longest, coldest winter on record. Last summer's terrible heat wave was a distant memory. Back then it got so hot cows dried up and gave powdered milk and I fell into the worst hitting slump of my life. I didn't want that slump ever to come back, but I sure hoped the sun would.

Mr. Bones is my dog, a long-nosed, yellow-haired fur ball that strangers often mistake for a bandicoot. He likes to be petted and he likes to lick faces. At the moment, petting was out of the question, because he was completely encased in a green-and-red-tartan doggy coat. You could pet the coat but not Mr. Bones. The hideous garment was a Christmas present from my mother. It fitted him as snugly as batter on a corn dog. He was quite proud of his silly coat.

"What's next?" I asked, shaking my head. "Two little pairs of plaid galoshes?"

My dog wagged his tail some more and buried his snout in a snowbank.

I was standing with my pals from the Rambletown Rounders baseball team at the bottom of Windsock Mountain in the middle of yet another snowstorm. Windsock Mountain is Rambletown's ski area. It is really more of a big hill than a mountain. The wind part is accurate, though. It was blowing like stink out here, snow slicing sideways through the bitter air.

Rambletown is where I live with Mr. Bones and my mom and dad. When it isn't snowing, I play third base and bat cleanup for the Rounders. We're the reigning champs of the 10-to-12 division.

"Walloper!"

An elbow dug into my ribs.

"Get ready!" barked my best friend, stellar shortstop Stump Plumwhiff. "Here comes the next chair."

We backed into position, looking over our shoulders at the fast-approaching lift that would carry us to the summit.

Everybody on the team has a nickname. Mine is the Great Walloper, on account of I like to wallop the hide off the ball. My real name is Banjo Bishbash. Banjo H. Bishbash, if you want to be particular. The *H* stands for "Hit." Aside from my mom and dad and some teachers, no one much uses my real name. Technically, my parents don't really use it either. They tend to call me Banjie. You can see why I prefer the Great Walloper. Walloper for short.

Except, the way this winter was going, it looked as if I would never again wallop another tater. Winter had dragged on for so long, we had run out of months for it. It had eaten up January, February, and March like a hungry man eats flapjacks. It was still going strong when April rolled around. Deep snow covered the ground like a centipede. You couldn't keep track of all the feet.

An empty double chair swung around on its cable, and I hopped aboard next to Stump. He was also pretty decent on a snowboard.

"Come on, boy!" I shouted.

Mr. Bones took a running leap and landed in my lap, his tail wagging a mile a minute where it stuck out at the back of his ugly coat. He loved chairlifts. He loved riding them to the top of a mountain almost as much as he loved bombing back down with me on my board.

We began our long, cold sweep up the hill.

Sharing the chair in front of us were pitcher Slingshot Slocum and center fielder Gasser Phipps. Directly behind us were first baseman Gilly Wishes and second bagger Ellis "the Glove" Rodriguez. The rest of the guys—catcher Tugboat Tooley, left fielder Ducks Bunion, right fielder Ocho James, and pinch hitter Kid Rabbit Winkle—were scattered over the ski area like sprinkles on an ice-cream cone.

Stump shivered and pulled his baseball cap down low on his head. Stump never went anywhere without his baseball cap. Even in the middle of the coldest winter on record, it was the only kind of hat he wore. His ears were redder than strawberries. They were, in fact, as red as his stand-up hair. Stump was self-conscious about his hair. This was one reason he never took off his baseball cap.

"Why don't you put on your helmet?" I asked.

"It just makes my ears colder." He grunted. "I'll put it on when we get to the top."

"You should wear a winter hat," I suggested.

"Don't like hats." Stump grunted. "Only like caps."

"You're crazy," I said.

"Crazy fast, you mean. You'll be eating my spray all the way down."

"Whatever," I said.

As the chair soared up the slope, I gazed down at the frozen landscape below and wondered when winter would finally end and baseball season would begin.

Winter had been going on for so long that it made a boa constrictor look short. Just as spring vacation rolled around, when the daffodils should have been in full bloom and the Rounders should have been getting ready for our season opener, the mayor had come on TV and told us all to turn back our calendars to January.

"No sense in wasting a good spring on such lousy weather," he said.

6

"January!" I had shouted to Mr. Bones. "We can't go back to January! Opening day is almost here. We're supposed to play the big, mean Hog City Haymakers."

Yep.

Those very same Haymakers.

The hard-charging, homer-hitting team we had beaten to win the championship the previous summer.

What a game!

Maybe you've heard about it?

Flicker Pringle, the Haymakers' ace fire-baller, had been one strike away from pitching the first perfect game in the history of baseball. The Rounders had been down to our last hope: me. And a slim hope it was. I'd been swinging the bat like a wet noodle ever since the start of a wicked heat wave. Then, out of the blue, lightning struck. I clobbered a walk-off homer to win the pennant.

My friends and I replayed the game in our heads all winter long. Now we were eager to get back out on the field and start playing again for real. With actual wooden bats and genuine, cowhide-covered baseballs. Only, the lousy weather wouldn't let us.

Well, I could complain all I wanted, but nothing I said was going to have any effect on the weather. Mother Nature was like a traffic light. She changed all the time, but only when she was ready. You just had to wait her out.

Which was how Stump and I found ourselves on a chairlift on the last Friday of spring vacation, bouncing toward the top of Windsock Mountain, snowboards strapped to our feet, Mr. Bones snuggled between us on the icy seat. When by all rights we should have been taking batting practice at Rambletown Field.

★ CHAPTER 2 ★

As we reached the summit, Mr. Bones sprang from the chair and bounded down the icy ramp that led to the slopes. Stump and I slid off our seats and glided after him to where Slingshot and Gasser were studying a big wooden trail map planted in the snow like a billboard.

"What looks good?" I asked.

Slingshot pointed at a jagged line on the map.

"We could take a crack at Darkness Falls," he said with a grin.

In spite of myself I gulped.

Darkness Falls is legendary. It is rated double black diamond. Which means it is the steepest, fastest, altogether hardest kind of ski trail. It plunges to the bottom of Windsock Mountain like a frozen waterfall, a series of heart-stopping drops interrupted occasionally by snow-covered boulders. Or so I had heard from older kids. I'd never actually braved Darkness Falls myself.

None of us had.

"What's up?" asked Gilly Wishes as he and the Glove coasted over from the lift. Gilly was on a snowboard. Glove wore skis.

"We were just picking which trail to take," explained Gasser Phipps. "Slingshot suggested Darkness Falls."

Glove's and Gilly's eyes got as big as Whoopie Pies.

"Just an idea," said Slingshot. "But we've been riding this mountain all winter. And we've conquered every single trail at least ten times. . . ."

"Every trail except one," added Stump.

"Exactly," said Slingshot. "Darkness Falls has been the elephant in the room."

"The what in the where?" I asked.

"The elephant in the room," explained Slingshot. "A thing that nobody wants to admit is there, except it's too big to ignore."

"I don't know what it's like at your house," cracked the Glove. "But we don't have any elephants at home. Chairs, tables, beds. That kind of thing. Definitely no elephants."

"It's an expression." Slingshot sighed. "Who's up for it?"

As we hemmed and hawed, Gilly's bright orange parka burst into song: *The 1812 Overture.* It's a noisy classical song with cannons that's often played during Rambletown's Fourth of July fireworks.

Real fireworks would have been nice. They would have meant summer was here at last.

Gilly unzipped his pocket and pulled out a cell phone. He flipped it open, and *The 1812 Overture* stopped playing as suddenly as it had started.

"Gilly Wishes here," he said into the mouthpiece. "My wish is your command. Oh, hey,

Tugboat. What's up?"

Gilly pulled the phone away from his ear. "Tugboat's already at the bottom with Ocho, Ducks, and Kid Rabbit. You'll never guess which trail they took."

I had the distinct feeling we would guess.

"I don't believe it," said the Glove.

Tugboat's tiny, excited voice spilled out of Gilly's phone.

"Put him on speaker," said Slingshot.

Gilly pressed a button and Tugboat's voice got big.

"We did it!" he exulted. "It was insane! You guys HAVE to go for it! You don't know what you're missing!"

"Thanks for sharing," Gilly said. "Save us a seat in the lodge. We'll be down pronto." He zipped the phone back into his pocket.

"So what do you think?" asked the Glove.

"I think we don't have a choice," said Gasser with a grin. "I think we've got to take Darkness Falls."

"I was afraid you were going to say that," I

said, snapping my goggles into place.

Stump strapped on his helmet.

Mr. Bones danced excitedly on his hind legs, nipping at the snowflakes that fluttered around us like popcorn in a popper. I would have laughed, except my stomach hurt too much.

It felt like the lid of a pickle jar. Tight.

Really, really tight.

"What are we waiting for?" Stump asked. "It's not getting any warmer up here."

With that he shot away. In a second he was twenty feet below us. Two seconds after that and he was gone, obliterated from view by the falling snow.

Slingshot went next, flashing a quick thumbs-up before scooting over the edge.

"Showtime!" said the Glove, clattering away behind Slingshot.

Gilly followed, leaving only me and Gasser.

"After you," the center fielder said.

"No, no, after you," I replied, edging behind him. "I insist."

"Age before beauty," he shot back.

"Rock paper scissors?" I suggested.

I played rock. Gasser draped me with paper. I went next.

"Ready, boy?" I asked.

Mr. Bones stepped on to my board, tucking himself under the bridge of my legs. I squeezed my knees against his sides, gave him a quick pat for luck, and let gravity work its magic.

Away we went. Trees flashed past. Boulders. Then everything ran together in a blur of speed.

We hit a bump and the ground dropped away like a trapdoor. We hurtled through space, weightless as astronauts. With no snow to rattle over, my board fell silent. The only noise was the wind in my ears and a faraway roar that sounded like a train howling through a tunnel.

Soon I realized that the roar came from me. I was screaming at the top of my lungs, a wordless, adrenaline-fueled howl.

I was still shouting when the woods opened,

14

revealing Windsock Mountain's wide-open base area. Down near the lodge, a group of small hemlock trees swayed in the breeze. As we rocketed toward them, I saw that they weren't trees at all. They were the guys. They waved madly as we sliced through the air like a couple of genies riding a runaway magic carpet.

We landed ten feet in front of them, throwing up a big cloud of snow, and skidded to a stop close enough to shake hands.

Mr. Bones stepped off the board as if it was no big deal. Like flying was something he did every day. I lay down and stretched full-out in the snow. It felt good to get reacquainted with planet Earth.

My eyes watered. My legs quivered. But I was smiling. At least I think I was. I couldn't tell for sure, because my face had less feeling than a block of ice.

"That," I panted, "was sick!"

A second later the sound of the roaring train returned. This time it came from Gasser.

Looking up, I saw him shoot out of the woods as if he'd been launched from a cannon.

"It's a bird!" cried Kid Rabbit as Gasser soared toward us.

"It's a plane!" chimed in Ducks Bunion.

"It's super center fielder," we all sang out together.

Gasser grabbed the tail of his board and waggled it stylishly. Then he tucked his head and went into a forward roll, just like something you'd see the Flying Tomato do.

He almost made it too.

Almost nailed his landing.

In horseshoes, Gasser's touchdown might have been worth a point. But close doesn't count in snowboarding. Close in snowboarding is about as useful as a flat tire in the Indy 500.

Gasser struggled to swing his board beneath him. The ground rushed up to meet him. It was a sprint to the finish between Gasser and the ground.

The ground won.

Gasser hit once, hard, like the first big skip a flat stone makes when you skim it across a pond. A series of smaller bounces followed as he tumbled sideways across the landing area.

Gravity 1, Gasser 0.

"Ouch!" said Ocho James, speaking for all of us.

We raced after our friend and teammate. When we caught up to him, he was lying motionless on his back in the snow.

His two gloved fists shot in the air.

"Yes!" he exclaimed.

"Dude!" I exclaimed as Mr. Bones gently licked his face. "Are you all right?"

"Actually, no," he replied. "I did something to my leg. I'm going to need some help here."

★ CHAPTER 3 ★

I looked out the kitchen window. Fat snow-flakes swirled through the gray sky.

"Rats," I said to Mr. Bones, who responded by wagging his tail happily. One thing about Mr. Bones, he was naturally optimistic. It would take a lot more than lousy weather to make him sulk. I wish I could've said the same about myself.

Today was Saturday. A week from now baseball season was supposed to begin. In fact, it was supposed to have begun already. Opening day had been postponed three times. According to the latest revised team schedule hanging on the refrigerator, the Rambletown Rounders were going to play the Hog City

Haymakers in a week.

Yeah, right. And pigs were going to fly.

"Rats," I said again. Mr. Bones wagged his tail some more.

My dad came into the kitchen. He wore a blue bathrobe over brown paisley pajamas and a pair of furry old slippers. The pajamas looked like something squirrels would use to build nests. The slippers looked worse. Like maybe actual squirrels.

"Morning, sport," he greeted me, rubbing sleep out of his eyes. "Had any breakfast yet? How about an omelet?"

One thing you should know about my dad: he loves to cook omelets. Some people like to play golf. Some do crossword puzzles. Others collect baseball cards or dress up like Civil War soldiers for fun. One of my dad's hobbies is cooking omelets. I have to admit, he is good at it. His omelets are the best I've ever tasted. And by far the biggest I've ever seen. The size of snow tires.

"Sure," I said as he rummaged around in the fridge.

Dad pulled out a carton of eggs, a brick of cheddar cheese, a carton of milk, a package of ham, and an armload of sweet peppers in the colors of the flag of Bolivia: red, yellow, and green.

"So," he asked over the sizzle of melting butter, "how's Gasser?"

"Broken leg," I said. "The doctor says he'll be out for the season. If we have a season, that is."

"Poor kid. What rotten luck."

"He says the leg doesn't actually hurt too much. If fact, he seems to be kind of enjoying himself at the hospital."

"Really? What's to like about hospitals?" my dad asked as he started dicing peppers. He chopped so fast, he would put a Marine Corps barber to shame. Bits of vegetables flew all over the place.

"Comic books," I explained, smiling at the

20

memory of Gasser in the hospital. "And ice cream."

After Gasser's snowboarding accident the day before, the whole team had visited him in the hospital. We'd found him propped up in a mechanical bed with a big stack of comic books by his side and a bowl of ice cream in front of him. Despite the heavy cast on his leg, he had been grinning as if he'd just heard the funniest joke in the world.

"What's so humorous about a broken leg?" asked Tugboat.

"The humerus is an upper arm bone," said Slingshot. He wanted to be a doctor one day. "The major bones of the leg are the femur, the tibia, and the fibula."

"The broken leg stinks," said Gasser. "It's the fibula. But this place isn't half bad."

He showed us a special button on a cord by the side of his bed. He said he could press it whenever he wanted and a nurse would appear with a snack.

By way of demonstration, he hit the button. Somewhere out in the hall, a bell sounded. Seconds later, a nurse dressed in light blue scrubs poked her head into the room.

"Everything all right?" she asked.

"May I have some ice cream?" Gasser asked politely. "Strawberry this time, please."

"But, Mr. Phipps," she said, "you've already eaten three bowls."

"I'm still hungry though," Gasser said. "And my leg is starting to ache a little bit."

"Hmmm," said the nurse. "That's no good, is it. I'll see what I can do."

She turned briskly and disappeared down the hall.

I have to say, we all had been very impressed.

"It's better than chicken pox," Gasser gloated. "It doesn't even itch." He eyed the fiberglass cast that covered his leg from ankle to knee. "At least, not yet it doesn't."

One at a time, all the Rounders had signed

the cast and wished Gasser luck. He assured us he'd be home in a day and on the bench for every game of the coming season.

The aroma of melting cheese and frying ham began to fill the kitchen. Mr. Bones sat by my side, intently eyeing Dad as he worked at the stove. From time to time the dog's tail wiggled and he licked his chops.

"Voilà," said Dad. He clicked off the burner and slid his creation out of the frying pan and onto a waiting platter.

"Yum," said my mom, arriving at the table just as breakfast did. "Your father makes the world's best omelets."

"Definitely the biggest," I said.

"One Bolivian Special coming right up," crowed Dad.

We'd learned about Bolivia in geography class. The South American country was about the size of California and Texas combined. It had once been part of the Inca empire. Spanish was one of the official languages. There were a lot of llamas. That was about all I knew about Bolivia.

Dad said, "Red, yellow, and green peppers, *con queso.*"

"And *jamon*," I added, saying the Spanish word for "ham."

"Delicious in any language," my mom said, tucking into a wedge of omelet.

Dad beamed.

"Eat up," he said. "There's plenty." He shuffled off to get dressed, his squirrelly slippers sweeping the floor like dust mops.

"I'll say there's plenty," I said. You could have fed a crew of lumberjacks on that tire of an omelet. When it came to giant-sized breakfasts, Paul Bunyan had nothing on my dad.

Mom and I ate. Mr. Bones peered longingly up at us from beneath the table. Outside the window, snow kept coming.

I wanted to be swinging a bat, hitting fastballs and deep drives. Making double plays and stealing bases. All that good stuff.

"I wish you boys would be more careful," Mom said between bites. Mom could be like that. Saying things out of the blue. I guess all moms could.

"Huh?" I said. My mind was still on baseball.

"Gasser's very lucky," Mom said.

"What's so lucky about a broken leg?" I asked. "Besides ice cream and comic books?"

"I mean, he could have been hurt even worse than he was, Banjie. He's fortunate the only thing he's missing is the baseball season."

"If we ever have a baseball season." I sighed.

★ CHAPTER 4 ★

After breakfast I cleared the table and loaded the dishwasher. Juice glasses went into the top rack, plates went into the bottom rack, and scraps of food went into Mr. Bones's dinner bowl.

He licked my face gratefully, then bounded over to chow down.

He was still eating when the phone rang. I dried my hands on my shirt and picked up the receiver.

"Hello?"

"Walloper," said the caller eagerly. "Are you ready for some baseball?"

It was Lou "Skip-to-My-Lou" Clementine,

manager of the Rambletown Rounders baseball team.

Before I could answer, he said, "Good! I knew you would be. Today's the day. We're finally going to have our first practice!"

"Um, Skip," I said, "are you near a window?"

"Sure. Why?"

"Take a look outside. There's ten feet of snow on the ground and more falling."

"I know it," he said cheerfully. "What a winter!"

"Skip, how in the world can we practice baseball in all that snow?"

"We'll figure out something," he said. "The fact of the matter is, we've got no choice. The league office just called. You know we're scheduled to take on big, mean Hog City next Saturday in the season opener! The game has already been put off more times than a second-hand coat. The league is not going to postpone it any longer. One way or another, we're going to play ball."

"But Skip," I protested, "we'll be lumbering around out there like polar bears. Have you ever seen polar bears play baseball?"

"Well, as a matter of fact, I haven't. I saw a regular black bear ride a unicycle one time, but I've never seen any kind of bear play baseball."

"Exactly," I said. "Because they can't."

"Enough about bears," said Skip Lou. "We should be thinking about the Haymakers."

"What's the difference, Skip?" I asked. Our archrivals are as big as grizzlies. Some of them are just as hairy, too.

Skip said something in reply, but I missed it. I was too busy thinking about the Haymakers. It is very unusual to see a bunch of sixth graders with full beards and mustaches. But the Haymakers are anything but ordinary. They are the biggest, meanest, scruffiest collection of players I'd ever seen. And they are good.

Really good.

Of course, we were no slouches either. We

were the reigning champs, after all.

"We need to practice," Skip said.

"No kidding," I answered. "I feel like a beat-up old car. That's how rusty I am."

"I hear the Haymakers have been going at it for a month," Skip said. "They're so eager to win back the pennant, they went through spring training in snowshoes."

"We've got a lot of catching up to do," I said.

"One o'clock sharp," Skip said.

"I'll be there," I promised.

"One other thing," Skip said before hanging up.

"What's that?"

"Bring a shovel. Bring two if you've got them."

Later that day, I put on my Inuit parka and my ski hat and my down-filled mittens and laced up my mukluks. Then I bundled Mr. Bones into his silly doggy coat.

"You've got a perfectly fine, natural coat

of thick fur," I pointed out as I zipped him up. "Why in the world you'd ever want to cover it with this plaid monstrosity, I'll never know."

I grabbed a snow shovel off the front porch, and we trudged across Rambletown to the ball field. It was like walking through Santa's village. Snowdrifts buried houses up to the eaves. You expected to see reindeer zipping through the air.

"On Donner," I called. My dog cocked his head at me as if I was crazy. "What?" I asked. "You might as well be a reindeer in that getup. No self-respecting dog would be caught playing dead in such a coat."

To let Mr. Bones know I was just kidding, I tossed a snowball for him to chase. He caught it on the fly and ate it.

When we got to the park, the whole team was gathered on the frozen tundra of what was once a baseball diamond. Everybody, that is, except Gasser Phipps. I wondered if he'd gotten tired of ice cream yet. Just the thought of it made me shiver. From where I was standing, the whole world looked like a big scoop of vanilla.

Mr. Bones and I greeted the guys: Slingshot. Ducks Bunion. Ocho James. Kid Rabbit. Stump. Tugboat Tooley. Gilly Wishes and his kid brother, Billy. The Glove. And, of course, Lou "Skip-to-My-Lou" Clementine.

Standing next to Skip was a tall guy in a red hat with big earflaps. I didn't recognize him.

"Welcome back, team," said Skip Lou, his breath puffing white in the frigid air. "It's been a long winter. But now it's high time for baseball. We're going to have to dig out the field to play, of course. Before we do, I want to introduce our newest teammate."

The tall guy in the red hat with earflaps smiled shyly.

"This here is Orlando Ramirez," said Skip. "He can catch anything that moves, and he's got a cannon for an arm. He'll be patrolling center field while Gasser mends. Orlando's family just moved to town. He starts school with you guys on Monday."

In addition to being coach of the Rounders, Skip Lou was the music teacher at Rambletown Elementary School. I guessed that was how he knew about Orlando and his family. Skip played clarinet like nobody's business.

We all welcomed the new kid to Rambletown and to the Rounders.

"Where did you move from?" I asked.

"Florida," Orlando said.

"Cool!" Billy Wishes gushed. "Like near Disney World? Orlando from Orlando?"

Billy once won a trip to Disney World for himself and his whole family. He really wanted to go back sometime. Given how lucky he was, I didn't doubt he would.

Orlando shook his head. "Farther north," he said. "Up around Jacksonville."

"You ever play snow baseball in Florida?" I asked, looking across our field.

"No, I haven't." Orlando laughed. "I've never

even been sledding. I have ice-skated though."

"In Florida?" Ducks asked, astonished.

"Sure. There's an indoor rink near where I lived. I used to go there all the time. I love to skate."

"That's good," said Ducks. "The way this winter is hanging on, we may have to change over into a hockey team." He nodded toward the field. "Just flood it and turn the outfield into a rink."

"I like winter," Orlando said. "It's . . . it's . . ."

"Cold," said Slingshot. "That's what it is. Cold and stubborn. It's like a rash that just won't go away. Personally, I think Florida sounds awesome. I bet you played baseball year-round."

Orlando nodded. "Even during Christmas vacation we went to the batting cages," he said. "In shorts and T-shirts."

"Chipper Jones is from Florida," chimed in Stump, our resident expert on the life stories and career stats of major-league players. "All that sunshine is a huge advantage. In Florida, players never have to shovel the diamond. So, are you any good?"

Stump never was shy about getting right to the point.

"Pretty good, I guess," Orlando muttered.

"You have a nickname?" asked Ducks Bunion, tactfully changing the subject.

"Some people call me Or," our new center fielder admitted.

We all considered this bit of information. Or didn't seem like much of a nickname. It didn't seem complete. "Or what?" you wanted to ask. "Or else?"

"I was thinking of something a little more colorful," said Ducks, whose actual name was Thomas. He'd been called Ducks since he was a baby, because he'd waddled like a duck when he was learning to walk. "Nicknames are kind of a tradition with the Rounders. Are you cool with that?"

"I wouldn't mind a nickname at all," said

Orlando. "It's just that nobody has ever been able to come up with one that stuck."

"We'll think of something," Ducks promised.

We grabbed our shovels and spread out across the diamond. We cleared big patches of ground, piling snow behind the foul lines. While we worked on the diamond, two town plows showed up and began removing snow from the outfield. The huge mounds they piled up at the edge of the field looked like jagged mountains.

Mr. Bones climbed to the top of the range and slid down on his belly.

At least somebody enjoyed the snow.

★ CHAPTER 5 ★

After the plows drove off, we started warm-up drills. In that cold, warming up was harder than a cement bed. We tried doing jumping jacks, but our bulky winter jackets and heavy boots made it almost impossible to get off the ground. Running the bases wasn't much better. It was hard to get any traction. We'd cleared away a lot of snow, but a hard-packed layer of it still coated the diamond. Running on it felt like a bad dream where something is chasing you, but no matter how hard you pump your legs you can't gain any speed. If we ever had to wear our full winter outfits in an actual game, we could forget about stealing any bases. Slow as we were going, we wouldn't even be able to borrow them.

"Good enough," Skip Lou said after about fifteen minutes. "Let's try some fielding drills. Everybody take your positions. The play will be at first base."

He stood at home plate and hit baseballs for us to catch. He hit one after another. Pop-ups, grounders, line drives, high bouncers, Texas leaguers, cans of corn. We bumbled around like a bunch of clumsy snowmen trying to catch them. Most got past us. When someone did make a stop, the throw to first was usually terrible. It was hard to throw accurately with a mitten on your hand. You couldn't get any feel for the ball.

"Not bad, not bad at all," Skip Lou called encouragingly as Stump muffed a grounder, then picked up the ball and fired it about a mile over Gilly's head at first.

Skip smacked a long fly ball toward center field.

Orlando Ramirez set off after it. On the tamped-down layer of snow left behind by the plows, he ran like a newborn colt, loose and skittery, every step a learning experience. His legs slipped in all directions. Gradually, he found his balance and gained some footing. Once he did, his legs started pumping up and down like pistons, and he gathered a head of steam.

"The kid's got wheels," Slingshot said approvingly as Orlando shot across the outfield. "I'll bet he really flies on grass."

Orlando raced under the ball and made a fantastic catch. Then he tried to stop running. He dug in his heels, but it didn't take. The hardened crust of snow was too slippery. He kept right on going, slip-sliding away at breakneck speed.

"Look out!" I yelled from third base. "Look out for the wall!"

The whole team held its breath.

Mr. Bones came over and stood beside me. That short-legged, long-nosed, yellow-haired fur ball liked to be petted and liked to lick faces.

He did not like to see people barrel into walls. He hid his face behind my knees.

Sha-bam!

Orlando smashed into the boards like a runaway train. Jarred loose by the massive collision, chunks of snow and ice crashed down from atop the wall and exploded on the frozen ground like bombs.

"Orlando!" I shouted.

Our new center fielder lay in a heap at the base of the outfield wall.

I sprinted toward him. At least I tried to sprint. With my winter coat and boots weighing me down, it felt as if I was wallowing in quicksand. The whole team struggled along behind me.

By the time we reached Orlando, he was sitting up. The ball was still in his glove. Somehow he had managed to hold on to it. He looked woozy. You could practically see stars dancing around his head, like in a cartoon.

"Yowch," he said.

"Are you all right?" I panted, crouching down next to him.

"I'm dizzy," Orlando complained. "I feel like I just ran into a wall."

I frowned.

"You did just run into a wall," I pointed out.

"Now why in the world would I do something like that?" he asked.

He was woozier than I thought.

Mr. Bones wiggled over and licked Orlando's face. He covered his cheeks and chin and nose and mouth with slobbery kisses.

"Pffft," said Orlando. He scratched Mr. Bones behind his ears.

Mr. Bones wagged his tail and licked faster.

Orlando slowly got to his feet. He brushed snow off his pants and coat. He looked as wobbly as a house of cards.

"Hold on there, Sport," said Skip Lou. "Let me take a look at you."

Skip took Orlando's hands and peered into his eyes. Orlando looked back at him.

"Do this for me, will you?" Skip asked, letting go of Orlando.

He spread his arms wide and touched first his left index finger, then his right to his nose. Without hesitating, the center fielder did the same.

"I feel fine, Coach," he said.

Skip nodded. "You look okay too," he said.

Suddenly, Stump pounded his fist into his big fielder's mitt.

"I've got it," he shouted as though the shortstop was about to make a catch.

We all looked at him. There was nothing to catch.

"What have you got?" we asked.

"Dizzy!" he said triumphantly.

"Why are you dizzy?" our pitcher, Slingshot Slocum, asked. "You didn't run into anything. Orlando did."

"No," shouted Stump. "Dizzy. It can be Orlando's nickname! Because he knocked himself dizzy. Plus, it's a great baseball name.

There's a Hall of Famer named Dizzy Dean."

We all thought about it for a minute. Upon reflection, it didn't seem like such a good nickname. The poor guy had run smack into a hard wooden fence at about sixty miles an hour. Calling him Dizzy added insult to injury. It wasn't much better than calling somebody Fat Lip or Shiner or Bloody Nose. Plus, "dizzy" kind of meant "scatterbrained."

Orlando didn't strike me as dizzy. He just seemed as if he didn't have any brakes.

He hung his head. Obviously he didn't like the sound of Dizzy.

"No offense, Stump," I said, "but I think we can do better. It's not like Orlando's always dizzy or anything. He seems pretty sane to me. Running into walls is kind of nuts, I guess, but that's more the field's fault than his."

All the guys murmured in agreement.

"Not to mention," said Ocho, "Dizzy Dean was a pitcher. He was a strike-out artist for the St. Louis Cardinals. He once whiffed Joe DiMaggio four times in a single game.

Orlando's not a pitcher."

"Hmmm," said Stump. "You have got a point there, Ocho."

Orlando smiled with relief. He assured us he felt fine. We all started walking slowly across the frozen field, picking our way between snowdrifts.

"How about Crash?" suggested Kid Rabbit Winkle.

"Splinter?" asked Ducks. "On account of that wooden fence is full of splinters."

"Train Wreck?"

"Ice Foot?"

"Battering Ram?"

"The Human Eel!" blurted the Glove as we reached the edge of the infield. He smiled as if he'd just won a pie-eating contest.

"The Human Eel?" I asked. "What in the world does that mean?"

"It means he's slippery," the Glove crowed. "Just like an eel! Get it? Because he slipped all over the outfield?"

We all stopped walking.

Orlando frowned. His shoulders slumped. You could tell he was thinking about what it would be like to go through life being called the Human Eel. How your friends and family would shudder every time you got your name in the paper or anything. How strangers would be scared of you. People who weren't afraid would just think you were weird. When you got right down to it, not a lot of people liked eels. Eels were kind of gross.

It was Tugboat who broke the silence this time.

"Nope," he said. "It's the field that's slippery, not Orlando. Besides, he's skinny, but he's not that skinny. A person would have to be super-skinny to go by the name of the Human Eel."

"And superslimy," added Billy Wishes.

Again, Orlando breathed a sigh of relief.

We started to take our positions in the field, but Skip Lou waved us off.

"That's enough for today," he said. "We've already got one center fielder in the hospital.

We don't need to send another one there."

He was right. We didn't need that at all. What we needed were dry clothes and steaming mugs of hot chocolate.

"Let's try again tomorrow," Skip said. "Same time, same place. Meantime, pray for a heat wave."

On that cheerful note, practice ended.

CHAPTER 6

The next day was balmy. Almost tropical. The temperature got all the way up to freezing, and it didn't snow more than a foot or so.

Mr. Bones and I bundled into our winter gear. I grabbed my bat and my mitt and my shovel. We headed over to the ballpark. Today we were going to practice hitting. Hopefully, it would go better than yesterday's fielding.

Orlando was digging out the bases with the rest of the guys when Mr. Bones and I arrived. The town plows were again doing their best to make the outfield playable.

Mr. Bones ran right over and licked Orlando's face.

"How's the old bean, Orlando?" I asked.

Meaning his noggin. Calabash. Pumpkin.

You know, his head.

"Rock solid," he said. "Never better."

"Glad to hear it," I told him. "The wall looks pretty good too. I see it's still standing where you tried to knock it down."

I patted him on the shoulder to let him know I was just kidding.

Orlando smiled.

We cleared the field of the fresh snow.

"Spring is in the air," said Lou "Skip-to-My-Lou" Clementine.

"Sure it is," said Slingshot as he walked out to the mound. "It is somewhere. Just not here. Australia, maybe."

"Only six days until we take on those Hog City Haymakers," said Skip. "Cold and snowy or warm and sunny, it doesn't matter. In less than a week we finally play baseball."

Tugboat pulled his catcher's mask over his ski hat and crouched down behind home plate. Slingshot tossed him a few easy ones. Tugboat caught them and fired them back.

"Batter up," called Skip Lou.

That was me.

Billy Wishes handed me my favorite bat. A big, long, heavy Louisville Slugger. I rubbed the batboy's head for luck and stepped up to the plate.

"Nice and easy, Slingshot," said Skip.

The pitcher nodded and threw me a fat one right down the middle.

I gave it a clout. The bat buzzed in my hands like a swarm of angry bees.

"Yowza!" I bleated as the ball sailed foul and buried itself in a snowdrift down the left field line. I wasn't used to hitting in cold weather. It stung.

I called time-out and pulled a pair of puffy winter mittens over my thin batting gloves. Then I stepped up to the plate again. Slingshot tossed me another cream pie.

This time I really clobbered it. The bat still buzzed, but the mittens softened the pain from a furious sting to more of a fuzzy vibration. The ball soared into the outfield.

Deep center.

Orlando locked onto its flight and gave chase. Ten feet in front of the sturdy wooden fence, his path crossed that of the ball. He took wing and snapped it up in his glove midair like a bat devouring a mosquito.

Amazing catch! Highlight material. It should have been on SportsCenter.

Orlando landed on his feet.

He did not fall down.

But he didn't stop either.

He couldn't.

"Uh-oh," I said, hoping lightning wouldn't strike twice.

I held my breath. I closed my eyes.

Sha-bam!

Lightning struck twice. Rather, Orlando did. He slammed into the wall like a football player trying to barrel into the end zone.

The wall made like the Pittsburgh Steelers defense. It didn't budge an inch.

When the reverberations finally died down and the frozen earth stopped trembling, we ran out to check on Orlando. He lay on the ground not more than three feet from where he'd crashed the day before. Mr. Bones got there first. He licked Orlando's face. He wagged his tail and licked some more.

"Pfft!" said Orlando.

He sat up and scratched Mr. Bones behind his ears.

"Orlando," I said, puffing onto the scene. "We held ten bake sales and six car washes to raise the money to get this wall built. If you knock it down, we'll never get another. Are you all right?"

"I've taken bigger lumps falling out of bed," he said.

He got up and opened his glove. Nesting inside like a big, round egg was the ball.

If Orlando didn't knock himself goofy, he was going to be a really great center fielder.

Slowly, we all started walking back across the field.

"How about Two Time?" suggested Tug-boat. "On account of this is the second time he ran into the wall."

"Greased Pig," said Ducks. "Because he skitters all over the place like a greased pig at a country fair."

"Banana Peel."

"Wallbanger."

"Wrecking Ball."

"Superstar," said Billy Wishes. "On account of he makes super catches, then he sees stars when he runs into the wall."

We all stopped walking.

"Not bad," said the Glove. "Not bad at all."

Everyone agreed that Superstar had a certain ring to it.

But somehow it still wasn't quite right.

"A player can be a superstar," said Ocho. "And Orlando definitely can run and catch with the best of them. But can Superstar really be a nickname?"

"It's like I told you," Orlando said glumly. "No one has ever been able to pin a good one on me."

"Don't worry," we promised. "We'll come up

with a winner if it's the last thing we do."

One by one, we slapped Orlando on the back.

"Take it easy," we warned before scattering across the hard-frozen field to our own positions.

Ducks stepped up to the plate. Slingshot lobbed one easy pitch after another right over the middle of the plate. Ducks swung as if the ball was a piñata and if he smacked it hard enough it would split open and spill candy. He didn't manage to shatter any of Slingshot's batting practice tosses, but he did turn them around in a hurry. He lasered shots all over the field.

Then it was Gilly's turn. He too teed off on one fat pitch after another.

We all hit the ball pretty well. It was good to see the winter layoff hadn't damaged our swings.

Fielding was another story. All practice long, we struggled to catch the ball. We tripped and slipped and stumbled. None of us had much success staying upright. But no one had a harder time than Orlando. The kid from Florida ran down every long ball to center. And he plowed into the wall after every catch. He never dropped a single fly. But by the end of practice the wall looked like French toast. Battered.

And so was Orlando.

"That's enough," called Skip Lou after Orlando's tenth crash of the afternoon. "Let's call it a day."

Skip looked glum.

We all looked glum.

We were glum. Especially Orlando.

The season opener was fast approaching. If we didn't get better in a hurry, those Haymakers would lick us like a Popsicle. After a month of practicing in snowshoes, they knew how to get around on a treacherous field.

Orlando looked at his feet. His boots were about as useful for baseball as a pair of flip-flops.

Real flip-flops would have been nice. They would have meant the beach and hot sun and sand between your toes.

"Maybe I should try snowshoes like the Haymakers," he said. "These sure aren't working."

Snowshoes would have been nice. A dogsled team would have been better. We definitely needed to try something new. We couldn't afford to give the Haymakers any advantage. Those guys were so good, they could show up barefoot wielding broomsticks for bats and oven mitts instead of baseball gloves and still crush nine teams out of ten.

"Maybe you should just lay off a little bit," suggested Skip. "Don't try to catch every single ball hit to center field. If the ball is sailing toward the wall, pull up and play it on a carom."

Orlando turned as pale as the belly of a fish.

"But Skip," he gasped, horrified. "I'm a center fielder. I catch flies. It's what I do."

"I like your moxie, kid," said Skip. "It's your health that worries me."

"Not to mention the health of the wall," added Ducks with a grin.

With that, practice broke up. Vacation ended with it. In the morning, we went back to school. To tell the truth, I wasn't sorry about that at all. Between the weather, Gilly's accident, and our lousy performances on the ball field—if you could call a snowy wasteland a ball field—it had been the worst spring break on record.

Mr. Bones and I said so long to the guys and trudged home, into the teeth of a biting north wind.

★ CHAPTER 7 ★

Monday morning, Dad offered to make omelets for breakfast. I was tempted. Watching him cook was fun. It was almost as good as eating what he cooked. But I decided to have oatmeal instead. It seemed better suited to the weather. Gray and mushy.

Just like my mood.

Dad was disappointed. He couldn't get creative with oatmeal. Mr. Bones was even more upset. He lived for leftovers. My dad's omelets were so big, nobody could eat a whole one. There was always something left for Mr. Bones.

"I'll make it up to you, buddy," I promised.

"I'll take you for a walk after school, and you can show off your coat all over the neighborhood."

He perked up.

After breakfast I spent about an hour putting on my cold-weather gear. All the extra clothes I have to wear is one of the worst things about winter. I was sick and tired of the layers, the thick socks, the sloppy boots, the mittens that never seemed to get completely dry.

I trudged off to the bus stop feeling more wrapped up than a mummy.

A real mummy would have been nice. It would have meant Egypt, where I understood the weather was hot and dry.

The bus pulled up and I climbed aboard. It was about three-quarters full. Stump and Slingshot waved to me from a seat toward the middle. I slid behind them, next to my friend and classmate Gabby Hedron.

Gabby is a photographer and reporter. She covers school events and baseball for *The Rambletown Bulletin*, the local newspaper.

"Morning, everyone," I said as the bus rumbled off.

"You hear about the Haymakers?" Gabby asked. "They've been practicing in snow-shoes."

Gabby is the Rounders' number one fan. On her list of favorite things, the big, mean, hairy Hog City Haymakers ranked somewhere between bad breath and poison ivy. Maybe lower.

"I heard," I said.

"Why haven't you guys tried it?"

"Good question," I said.

At the next stop, Gasser hopped up the steps. Every eye was on him as he hobbled down the aisle on a pair of aluminum crutches.

"Gasser! Gasser!" kids yelled. "Did you really pull a double-front roll Flying Walrus? On Darkness Falls!"

"Triple." Gasser grinned gamely as he lowered himself into the empty seat across from Stump and Slingshot.

"Triple, my foot!" hooted Slingshot. "The only triple you scored was three scoops of fudge ripple ice cream in the hospital."

"Don't talk to me about it." Gasser groaned, suddenly looking as green as a dish of pistachio ice cream. "I don't want to see any more ice cream as long as I live."

The bus lurched ahead. Soon we reached the corner of Oxford and Riverview. Orlando stood amid iceberg-sized snowdrifts on the sidewalk. He was bundled in enough arctic gear to launch an expedition to the North Pole. If not for his familiar red hat with earflaps, I probably wouldn't have recognized him.

The door cranked open, and our new center fielder slowly climbed aboard. With his hat pulled low, he made his way nervously through the bus. Kids who hadn't met him, which was pretty much everyone, openly stared.

Orlando seemed relieved when he spotted Slingshot, Stump, and me. His face lit up like a video arcade under his red hat.

"That's the new center fielder, isn't it?" Gabby whispered. "I recognize him from practice."

"Orlando Ramirez," I told her. "He's like a frog. Expert at catching flies."

"I never saw a frog jump straight into a wall," Gabby said.

"You saw that?"

"I see everything the Rounders do," said Gabby. "It's my job."

"What's happening, Orlando?" I greeted him. "How many fingers am I holding up?" I flashed two.

"Cut it out, Walloper." He chuckled. "I can see just fine."

"Tell it to the outfield wall." Stump laughed. "Hey, Gasser, get your bum leg out of the way and make room for Orlando. He's on the team, you know."

"Pleased to meet you," said Gasser, pogoing out of his seat. "Slide in, why don't you? I need to sit next to the aisle so I can stretch out my leg."

Orlando scooted over beside the window, and Gasser plopped down beside him.

"So, you're the guy who's taking my place?" he asked.

"I guess so," Orlando said apologetically. "I mean, I didn't plan on replacing anyone. I just wanted to play baseball. I'm sorry about your leg."

"Don't worry about it. The doctor says the old peg will be fine. It just needs time to heal. You ever break anything?"

"I broke my wrist once," Orlando said as all the kids on the bus listened in. "Skateboarding."

Everybody nodded appreciatively. A skateboarding accident was cool. I could tell Orlando would be just fine at Rambletown Elementary.

Gabby leaned toward him and introduced herself.

"I write about the Rounders for the newspaper," she said. "We should talk."

Orlando smiled politely and nodded in an offhand way. All the attention seemed to make him uncomfortable.

Under normal conditions, either a broken leg or a new kid would totally dominate school news all by itself. To have both on the same day? That was like dessert after Thanksgiving dinner: almost too much of a good thing. Apple pie and pumpkin pie and ice cream and shortbread cookies and whatever crazy thing your great-aunt had dreamed up with Jell-O, whipped cream, and custard. A person hardly knew where to start.

But our first day back after vacation turned out to be anything but normal. Both Gasser and Orlando were dwarfed by a snow mountain.

Literally.

★ CHAPTER 8 ★

We saw the mountain for the first time when the bus pulled into the school parking lot. You could hardly miss it. The thing totally dominated the white winter landscape. It towered above the school grounds like a landlocked iceberg. If it had been an iceberg, forget about the *Titanic*. It was so big, it would've sunk Greenland.

As we drew into its enormous shadow, every kid fell quiet. The only sound at all was the thunk of dropping jaws as they hit the floor. A silent school bus was a strange and eerie thing. But compared to the snow mountain, a quiet school bus seemed normal.

"Holy Himalayas," Slingshot finally gasped.

Gabby whipped a camera out of her backpack and started snapping pictures through the window.

"Where on Earth did that come from?" Gasser wondered.

"I don't know," said Gabby. "But this is front-page stuff. Have you ever seen anything like it?"

"In my nightmares," said Stump. "It's so steep, it makes Darkness Falls look flat."

"Don't talk about Darkness Falls," said Gasser.

"The plows," Slingshot whistled. "They must have made it when they cleared the parking lot."

Of course! Slingshot was right. So much snow had fallen during spring vacation that the road crews had run out of places to put it. In pushing and piling it around the lot, they had created a giant, jagged peak that made Mount Everest look like an anthill.

"Wow," breathed Orlando, his eyes popping.

I could only imagine what he was thinking. Until very recently, this was a kid whose idea of an arctic environment was the ice cube tray in his freezer.

"And people say Florida is nuts," he muttered, shaking his head. "Just because you run across the occasional alligator."

The bus squeezed past the mountain and pulled up in the unloading area. Cars were backed up all the way to the main road. Out in front of the school building, Principal Gorton directed traffic.

Gabby turned and got a picture of the principal waving at the stream of vehicles trying to turn into the lot. She wore orange gloves and looked like she belonged on an airport runway landing jumbo jets. All she needed was a control tower. If she'd had one, maybe people would have paid more attention. As it was, cars jockeyed for position, horns blaring, as everyone tried to get a close-up view of

Rambletown's newest natural wonder.

The bus driver cranked the lever that opened the door. One by one, we filed down the steps. At the bottom, several teachers waited like prison guards. They guided us briskly to a shoveled walkway that led to the front doors of the school. Mounds of snow stood so high on either side that passing between them felt like walking along the floor of a canyon.

I turned and gazed over my shoulder at the mountain. More teachers were stationed around the base, making sure nobody got any bright ideas about climbing it. Someone had set up a few sawhorses to keep people away from the slopes. If they were real horses, I'm sure they would have bolted. One avalanche and they would be like pirate's treasure: buried.

On an icy ridge way up the steep slope, I swear I could just make out the profiles of four presidents. It was like Mount Rushmore, only the faces were different. I recognized John F. Kennedy right away. He's on a half-dollar my grandfather gave me for my birthday one year. But I wasn't sure who his three partners were.

The Mount Rambletown presidents were stone-cold huge. They also looked just plain cold.

Gabby snapped off a string of pictures.

"This is hot stuff," she exclaimed.

"Cold, you mean," I said.

"It's no fair," complained Stump, his voice echoing off the banks of snow that rose on either side of us.

"What's no fair?" asked Slingshot.

"All the barricades and stuff," Stump said, pointing to the mountain with disgust. "They sure know how to kill a good time around here. I would do anything to conquer that beast. There are probably ice caves to explore and everything."

"Definitely," agreed Gasser. "Unfortunately, I won't be climbing anything for a while." He raised a crutch and waved its rubber tip toward Mount Rambletown. "You guys'll have to go up without me and come back with a full report. I expect lots of pictures."

"Pictures are easy." Gabby smiled as we entered school. "Pictures we can do."

We started walking again. The bell would ring at any minute. Monster snow peak or not, none of us wanted to be late our first Monday back.

But Stump was right.

It isn't every day that a gigantic geologic formation appears practically in your own backyard. We were going to have to figure out a way to get around the security.

Somehow, some way, we needed to mount an expedition to the summit.

★ CHAPTER 9 ★

In Rambletown Elementary's wide entry hall, kids sloshed in every direction. The gray tile floor was slick from hundreds of pairs of slushy boots. You practically could have paddled a canoe on it, that's how wet the floor was.

Orlando hesitated among long glass cases full of school trophies. He seemed a little lost. Suddenly it occurred to me that he didn't know which way to go. The guys and I had bonded so quickly with Orlando at baseball practice that it was easy to forget our familiar old school was completely foreign to him.

"What room are you in, Orlando?" I asked.

There were two sixth-grade classes.

"Number twelve, I think," he said. "Mr. Sicko."

Gasser burst out laughing. "Mr. Swickle," he corrected. "Sicko. That's a good one. I'll have to remember that."

"Right," Orlando mumbled. "Mr. Swickle. That's what I meant to say."

"Cool," said Slingshot. "That means we're together. Follow us."

We started moving down the hall, and Orlando made like a baseball card. He joined the pack.

"Clear some space," Stump bellowed as we rounded a corner. "Wounded soldier coming through. Wounded solider. Make way!"

A group of younger boys moved aside to let us pass. When they saw Gasser swinging along on his crutches, their eyes widened.

"Hey, Gasser," called Joey Bing, a third grader. "I heard you jumped out of a heli-copter to the top of Windsock Mountain and landed in a pine tree. . . ."

"And there was a bear in the tree," chimed in Joey's friend Malcolm Krentz. "And you wrestled him to the ground. . . ."

"And you ended up going over Darkness Falls with the bear riding on the nose of your board," Joey continued.

"Backward!" finished Malcolm.

"Is it really true?" they asked hopefully.

Gasser leaned on his crutches. "Well, guys," he said slowly, "the truth is, it didn't happen that way. Not exactly."

The third graders' faces fell as if they'd been pushed over a cliff.

Stump flashed us a sneaky smile, then stepped forward. He slung his arm over Gasser's shoulders.

"Not at all," he said. "You see, the bear didn't jump on his board."

"It didn't?" Joey and Malcolm asked. They sounded like a couple of soda cans that had been tossed in a trash compactor: crushed.

"Nope," continued Stump. "It actually strad-dled Gasser's shoulders. Dude piggybacked that bear halfway down the mountain."

"Whoa!" said Joey.

"Awesome!" gushed Malcolm.

"That's why Gasser crashed," Stump went on with a gleam in his eye. "The bear covered his goggles with its paws, and Gasser couldn't see a thing. Hit a jump doing about seventy miles an hour. By the time he knocked the bear off his shoulders, it was too late: he was airborne and way off balance."

The boys were speechless.

"The rotten part of it, worse than the broken leg," added Gasser, playing along with Stump's crazy story, "is that the bear ran off with my goggles. They were brand-new, too." He swung down the hallway on his crutches. "You guys want," he called over his shoulder, "I'll let you sign my cast later."

We left Joey and Malcolm slapping high fives and continued to Room 12.

Mr. Swickle was copying a poem on the blackboard as we noisily entered.

"Ahh," said our teacher, turning, "I see the baseball contingent has arrived. With our new classmate in tow." The teacher smiled and nodded toward Orlando. "Why don't you show Orlando where to hang his coat, please, then take your seats and we'll get started."

I sneaked a quick glance over at Gasser. He looked as though he'd swallowed a gobstopper. His face was purple. I guessed he was thinking the same thing I was—Mr. Sicko!—and trying hard not to laugh. It wasn't fair, really. Mr. Swickle was a great teacher. Once the cat was out of the bag, though, there was no getting it back in. I knew that from now on Orlando's flub would always ring in my ears.

We led Orlando to the cubbies at the back of the room and found the one with his name on it. The tall, open lockers were arranged alphabetically by students' first names. Orlando's came just after Nick Boudreau's and right before

Penny Chen's. It was painted fire-engine red, like the others, and had hooks for hanging coats and backpacks, with an open space underneath for boots. Compared to all the others, Orlando's cubbie was clean and uncluttered. It seemed somehow a little sad, like a house with no one living in it.

At nine o'clock sharp, Mr. Swickle called the class to order.

"Before we get started with today's poem," he said, "I have a couple of important announcements to make. First, I'd like to welcome Orlando Ramirez. Please stand, Orlando."

Every head in the class swiveled around to stare at the new kid. Poor Orlando did his best impression of butter on a hot day. He melted. The guy was great in center field, but playing center of attention was a different story. He obviously hated it.

"Orlando's family just arrived from Florida," said Mr. Swickle. "I know I speak for the whole class when I say how pleased we are to have him. Let's give him a big, warm welcome to Room twelve."

Everybody clapped politely. Everyone, that is, except Stump. He cheered like he was at a ball game. "Or-lan-do! Or-lan-do! Or-lan-do!" he chanted, pumping his fist in the air. If he could have, I'm sure Stump would have done the wave.

Unfortunately, it takes more than one person to do the wave.

"Second order of business," continued the teacher. "Undoubtedly you will have noticed something new when you arrived at school this morning."

A murmur of excitement buzzed through the room.

"Yes, I refer to the giant mountain of snow heaped by plows during vacation. Word to the wise: do not even think about going anywhere near it. The mountain is off-limits. No one is to climb it, slide down it, build a snow fort on it, or otherwise have anything to do with it. In other words, pretend it isn't there."

Stump raised his hand.

"Yes?" called Mr. Swickle.

"Are you saying we should treat Mount Rambletown like the elephant in the room?"

I snorted. Leave it to Stump.

Mr. Swickle leveled his gaze at my friend. "Elephant, tiger, great white shark, *T. rex*. Call it what you want. I'm saying, stay away from it. The consequences for not doing so, I am advised, will be severe. Does everyone understand?"

The class groaned in unison. We understood.

"Do you particularly understand, Mr. Plumwhiff?"

Stump made a "Who me?" face and held up his hands.

"Excellent," said Mr. Swickle.

★ CHAPTER 10 ★

"**L**et us now turn our attention to the blackboard," said Mr. Swickle. "You will notice where I have inscribed a poem for our mutual pleasure and enlightenment."

April is National Poetry Month. Mr. Swickle celebrated the occasion by starting every morning with a new poem. I guess it could have been worse. April could have been National Long Division Month or something.

Surprisingly, a few of the poems actually were okay. They hardly seemed like poems at all. The best ones used normal words that sometimes didn't even rhyme and they could be about almost anything you could think of. Such as jumping off a rope swing into a cool pond on a hot day.

A real hot day would have been nice. It would've melted the snow.

"As you can see, today's selection is called 'Father Time Is Coming' by the poet J. Patrick Lewis," Mr. Swickle said. "It's about a subject near and dear to many of our hearts—baseball. Who would like to read it?"

A half dozen hands shot into the air, including mine. I'd never heard of the poem, but I knew you couldn't beat the subject.

"Gabby? Excellent. Begin when you're ready."

Gabby stood at her desk and cleared her throat. "Father Time Is Coming,'" she read. "'Out of a windmill windup, the whipcord arm grooves a dartball.'"

I sat up a little straighter in my chair. In my head I could see the hurler whipping his pitch. I didn't know what a dartball was, but it sure sounded nasty. Gabby continued reading through a list of weapons this cool character had in his arsenal. Forget about ordinary fastballs and curves. The guy's stuff included the "two-hump blooper" and the "radioball"—you could hear it, but you never saw it. That last one reminded me of Flicker Pringle, star pitcher of the Hog City Haymakers. He whips the ball so hard it's nothing but a blur.

"'I'm Satchel,'" Gabby recited, reaching the poem's last line. "'I do as I do.'"

Suddenly the words made sense. A whole lot of sense. They were about the real-life, old-time ace Satchel Paige.

"Well done, Gabby," Mr. Swickle said. "Thank you." He walked around his desk and sat on the front edge. "Can anybody tell us anything about Satchel Paige?"

Immediately, Stump's hand shot up. Big surprise. His idea of a clever verse may have begun and ended with "He who smelt it, dealt it." But his knowledge of baseball was tops.

"He was a pitcher," Stump said. "Maybe the best ever."

"Very good." Mr. Swickle nodded. "Anything else?"

"Sure," continued Stump, warming up to his task. "Satchel started in the Negro Leagues. This was like eighty years ago, back when African Americans weren't allowed to play in the bigs. He had really nasty stuff. But nobody knew exactly how good he really was, because he couldn't pitch against major-league hitters. They finally found out after Jackie Robinson broke the color barrier in 1947. That's when African Americans entered the major leagues for the first time. The next year, Satchel joined the Cleveland Indians. He was an old man by then, like more than forty."

"Ancient," said Mr. Swickle. "Older than Methuselah."

"I don't know who this Methuselah character is," said Stump, frowning. "Did he play for the Reds maybe?"

"Never mind. A little joke," said Mr. Swickle with a twinkle in his eye. "Go on, Stump. You're doing great."

"Well, a lot of people figured major-league batters would knock Satchel down a notch or two. Plus, like you said, the guy was older than Methuseh-whoever. His best years were behind him. But Satchel rocked their world. He blew people away with these crazy pitches nobody had ever seen."

Slingshot raised his hand, and Mr. Swickle called on him.

"Satchel had names for all his pitches," the Rambletown pitcher said admiringly. "The poem talks about some of them. The looper, the drooper, the two-hump blooper."

"It sounds as though this guy had a lot of fun," Mr. Swickle observed.

"Nothing in the world is more fun than whiffing a batter," Slingshot said firmly. He would know. Our own ace pitcher had fanned more than his share.

"Why do you think the poet calls his poem 'Father Time Is Coming?'" asked Mr. Swickle.

"Easy," said Stump. "Because Satchel was so old."

"So, the best hitters in the world learned to respect Satchel?" Mr. Swickle asked.

"More than respect. They were awed. Yankee Hall of Famer Joe DiMaggio, he's in the poem, called him the best and fastest pitcher he'd ever seen," said Stump. "Satchel's enshrined alongside DiMaggio in Cooperstown now."

"Very impressive, Stump," said Mr. Swickle. "You sure do know your stuff."

"Got to," said Stump. "I'm a ballplayer. Need to know the history of my game."

"If only you approached regular history with the same diligence," Mr. Swickle said with a smile.

We all laughed. Stump's face turned as red as his stand-up hair, but he smiled too.

We spent another half hour discussing Satchel Paige and baseball and what it meant to be a hero. Every so often, I looked over at Orlando. His mouth hung open and his eyes bugged wide. Apparently they didn't cover baseball at his old school.

"When a rare individual like Satchel Paige comes along," said Mr. Swickle, "a Mozart, a Picasso, an Einstein, well, their extraordinary accomplishments seem to elevate the whole human race."

It was a pretty intense idea for a Monday morning. The first day back from vacation, no less. But I thought I understood what he meant. Just knowing that Satchel could do what he did, could overcome so many barriers and accomplish something great, it made you feel good inside. It made you feel hopeful and proud and amazed. To me, that's what the poem was about.

In any case, it was one of the best classes ever. I wished Mr. Swickle would give us more poems about baseball. It almost took my mind off the fact that Rambletown Field was still buried under ten feet of snow.

Almost.

Then I happened to glance out the window and catch a glimpse of Mount Rambletown. I couldn't be sure, but I thought one of the presidents winked.

Seeing that thing looming like a gigantic soft-serve ice-cream cone brought me back to reality in a hurry. It reminded me that we could gab about baseball all we wanted; but until the snow melted, the Rounders wouldn't be playing much of it.

Not very well we wouldn't.

★ CHAPTER 11 ★

My fears were borne out at practice the next afternoon.

Mr. Bones and I arrived at Rambletown Field at four o'clock sharp on Tuesday and immediately started shoveling snow off the diamond.

Again.

Or at least I did. Mr. Bones scampered up the heaps of snow piled around the edge of the infield and slid down on his belly.

"He should be in the Olympics." Gabby laughed, snapping away with her camera. "The bobsled. But that obnoxious plaid coat has got to go."

"Shhh! Don't let him hear you," I said. "He

doesn't know it's plaid. Dogs are color-blind."

"Ahhh," said Gabby. "That explains it."

She took another picture.

"Please don't put that in the paper," I begged.

Gilly Wishes showed up and helped me dig out third base. Then I helped him clear a path from home to first. The other guys worked to get the rest of the diamond into some kind of shape. The town plows had already visited the outfield, I could see, leaving behind their usual thin layer of snow.

As we shoveled, Skip Lou ambled about, giving encouragement. He stamped his boots on the frozen ground and slapped his thick gloves together.

"Fine afternoon for baseball!" he said unconvincingly. "What a great time of year. Excitement in the air, first game of the season only days away!"

I looked up at the sky. I didn't see any excitement in the air. The only thing I saw were snow flurries.

Skip smiled broadly and wandered away to greet the rest of the team.

Gilly and I exchanged perplexed glances. Poor Skip was in serious denial.

After we finished scraping snow off the field, practice began. The infielders started by tossing the ball around the horn. Having learned our lesson last week, we removed our winter mittens and wore only our baseball gloves. From the mound, Slingshot fired the ball home to Tugboat. The catcher squeezed the ball and whipped it to me at third. I quickly turned and gunned it to the Glove at second base, who flipped it to Stump, covering the bag. Stump relayed it to Gilly at first, who tossed it back to Slingshot. Then the whole thing started over again.

"Hot potato!" called Tugboat, scorching the ball to me. "Get rid of it fast."

A real hot potato would have been nice. It would've warmed up our cold, red hands.

Meanwhile, Skip Lou worked with the

outfielders. He stood at the edge of left field and hit flies to Ducks, Orlando, Ocho, and all-around back-up player Kid Rabbit. They raced to get under the ball and make the catch. Whoever snagged it on the fly scored a hundred points. The first player to get to five hundred would replace Skip at bat.

Skip smacked a long, high drive. The fielders took off after it, their scarves flapping in the wind like kite tails.

"I got it!" cried Orlando.

Running full tilt, he reached out with his glove. The ball settled into it as lightly as a bird returning to its nest. Then Orlando slammed on the brakes. If he had been a car traveling on a dry road, his tires would have laid down serious rubber. But he wasn't a car. He was a baseball player, sliding out of control across a slippery field toward a looming wall.

"Look out, Orlando!" I yelled from third.

Mr. Bones dashed over and hid his eyes behind my knees.

None of us could bear to look.

We didn't have to. Our ears told us all we needed to know.

Sha-bam!

Orlando had done it again. He had made a great catch and nearly killed himself doing it. Before we could run out to check on him, he popped up to his feet.

"I'm okay," he shouted. Grinning crazily, he fired the ball back to Skip.

"This is not good," muttered the Glove. "We need to figure out some way to help him."

"What we need," grumbled Tugboat, "is for winter to end and spring to begin. I don't know about you guys, but my hands are freezing."

As we talked, we heard a terrible whooping. Snowballs filled the air. A fat one nailed me square in the chest.

Yowch!

That smarted. Really smarted.

I turned to find out who had thrown it and saw a band of Vikings storming the field. Our field. The big, hairy marauders shouted war cries and fired snowballs every step of the way. Icicles dripped from their bushy mustaches and beards. Leading the charge was a tall warrior with a mean face and a meaner arm. He wound up and whistled a cold one inches over my head. I would've recognized that delivery anywhere.

It belonged to none other than Flicker Pringle, star pitcher of the Hog City Haymakers.

"Take cover," I shouted to the guys. "Defend our turf!"

"What turf?" the Glove asked. "All I see is snow."

"You know what I mean," I said as our rivals charged forward.

Dodging a storm of snowballs, we scrambled behind the mounded snowbank along the first baseline and swiftly packed a stockpile of ammunition.

"On three!" Slingshot yelled.

He gave the count, and we sprang out of our bunker and returned fire. Meanwhile, Kid Rabbit led a flanking movement from left field. As we blasted away, the outfielders maneuvered behind the Haymakers. The invaders had nowhere to hide. Our snowballs crashed down on them like meteors.

"You're just mad we beat you for the pennant," I shouted.

"That was last year," bellowed Flicker from atop the pitcher's mound. "This is now. You won't get lucky twice!"

Lucky! Luck had nothing to do with it. We'd beaten them fair and square.

His eyes were smoky and full of fire as he reared back and blasted another snowball my way. His long arm snapped like a whip. The frozen sphere sliced the cold air like a hot comet.

Holy hand grenades!

It was coming right at me!

I dropped behind the bank and tried to

get small. But the ball was coming too fast, a whizzing, dimpled blur with my name on it. I squeezed my eyes shut and prepared to meet my maker.

The icy blast never came.

Instead, a metallic clink rang out inches from my face. It sounded like an aluminum bat meeting a baseball.

When I opened my eyes, I was staring close-up at a metal tube. I blinked, and the object came into focus. It was Gasser's crutch. Gasser himself lay sprawled across the snow, the crutch extending from his outstretched arms. Right down by the tip was a big white blotch, the harmless remains of Flicker's snowball. Gasser had batted it away at the last second.

"Thanks, dude," I said. "I thought I was a goner!"

"No problem," he said. "These things are pretty handy."

We sprang up to return the volley, but the Haymakers had already pulled out of range.

They slipped safely through the gate, jeering all the way.

"See you Saturday, chumps!" yelled Flicker as he and his gang disappeared into the flakes swirling down from the cold, gray sky. "Expect a serious beating!"

Then they were gone.

And we were mad.

Really mad.

★ CHAPTER 12 ★

Splashed across the front of *The Ramble-town Bulletin* the next day was a picture of the snow mountain at school. While my mom and dad bustled in and out of the kitchen doing morning stuff, I sat down at the table with a bowl of Pirate Crunch cereal and looked at the paper. Gabby had gotten a really good shot. You could practically feel a cold wind whistling right off the page. Huddled together for warmth, the four blurry presidents glowered down from their icy heights.

"Check it out, Mr. Bones," I said. "How'd you like to snowboard down that?"

At the mention of snowboarding, he scampered into the mudroom and stood under the hook with his ugly coat hanging on it. His tail wagged like a metronome set on high.

"Sorry, pal," I said. "Not today. I've got school. Plus, this is one mountain we're supposed to stay away from. Principal's orders."

I turned back to the picture.

The caption said:

A mountain has arisen overnight in Rambletown. It's so big, it makes Alaska look small. Not to mention warm. Scientists are puzzled as to how the likenesses of four American presidents came to appear on the steep flank of our town's newest landmark.

"Mom," I said, slipping a piece of toast to Mr. Bones under the table. "Remind me again which presidents are carved into Mount Rushmore?"

"Washington, Jefferson, Roosevelt, and Lincoln." Mom ticked off the names. "Teddy

Roosevelt, that is. Not Franklin. Social studies assignment, Banjie?"

"Do these guys look like them?" I asked as Mr. Bones licked my hand.

"Which guys?" Setting her coffee mug on the table, Mom leaned over my shoulder and peered at the paper.

"Oh . . . my . . . goodness," she exclaimed. "What is that?"

"We call it Mount Rambletown. Principal Gorton says everybody has to stay off it."

"I should think so," Mom said. She leaned closer. "These are different presidents. It looks like John Adams, Franklin Roosevelt, John F. Kennedy, and . . . Who is that last one?"

My dad breezed into the kitchen, knotting his tie.

"What's so interesting?"

He leaned over Mom, who was still leaning over me. I felt like the front end of a collapsing Slinky.

"Ah," he said. "Mount Rushmore."

"Look closer," said my mom.

Dad bent closer, setting off a chain reaction. Another inch and I'd be snorting Pirate Crunch through my nose.

"How about some breathing room?" I hissed, bracing my hands against the edge of the wooden table. I felt like a glass of orange juice. Freshly squeezed.

Dad backed off a little.

"Wait a minute!" he exclaimed. "Is that Millard Fillmore, our thirteenth president? What's he doing up there? Where's George Washington?"

"It's not Mount Rushmore," I said to set my dad straight. "It's the snow heap at school. Read the caption."

Dad read.

"Jumping Jehoshaphat!" he blurted. "Right here in Rambletown? This thing could be huge."

"It is huge," I assured him. "It takes up

half the parking lot. The peak is shrouded in clouds."

"I mean, it's big news. When word gets out, people are going to want to see this thing. Tourists will come from all over."

"You're kind of crowding us, honey," Mom said. She slipped from between us like a tomato escaping from a sandwich. "I think that one on the end is Calvin Coolidge," she added. "Not Millard Fillmore."

"Really?" asked Dad. "I don't know. Franklin Pierce, perhaps? One of those obscure middle guys."

"Taft," I suggested.

Dad stepped over to the counter and popped some bread into the toaster. I took advantage of the elbow room to eat some cereal. With my mouth.

"William Howard Taft was gigantic," he said, shaking his head. "He was so fat, he once got stuck in his bathtub. Yep. Wedged himself in there like a cork. He was so big, he'd need his own mountain."

I tried to imagine someone getting wedged in a bathtub. Not a pretty picture. Even worse was what it would be like to haul the person out. One thing I knew for sure: I wouldn't want to be the one doing the pulling.

I turned to the sports section and found another article by Gabby. This one was about how the Rounders had opened spring training in a blizzard. Above the story was a picture. It showed Orlando barreling into the wall.

The caption said:

New Rambletown Rounders center fielder Orlando Ramirez really uses his head in the field. Mostly, he uses it to ram the outfield wall. It's a strange habit, but then there's nothing normal about playing baseball in the snow. Orlando just arrived in Rambletown from Florida. His previous idea of white stuff was fine sand on a sunny beach. He hopes this winter's record snow-fall melts by Saturday. That's when the Rounders kick off the season against the Hog City Haymakers. The wall hopes it melts, too. It's getting tired of Orlando's "heady" playing style.

"Way to go, Orlando." I chuckled to myself. One day of school under his belt and he's already famous.

I tossed aside the paper and stood up. It was time to meet the school bus. I pulled on my coat, said good-bye to my folks, and gave Mr. Bones a scratch behind his floppy ears. Then I headed out into the cold.

The big orange bus pulled into sight just as I got to the stop. I climbed up and took my usual seat next to Gabby, behind Stump and Slingshot.

"Did you know," I said by way of greeting, "that William Howard Taft was so fat he once got stuck in his bathtub?"

My friends looked at me as if I was speaking in tongues.

"Taft," I smugly explained. "The twenty-seventh president of the United States."

★ CHAPTER 13 ★

The bus barely managed to squeeze into the lot. Too many tourists crowded the school grounds. They'd ditched their cars by the side of the road and streamed forward on foot. Bundled from head to toe against the cold, hundreds stood gawking at Mount Rambletown. Parents of classmates, office workers who'd detoured past school on their way to their jobs, high school kids cutting class, nurses from the hospital. Most carried cell phones or video cameras. Those who weren't taking pictures of the snow peak took pictures of one another. Despite the frigid temperature, they all looked happy. Everyone laughed and pointed and clapped. And generally took up too much space.

"Yowza!" exclaimed Gabby. "Do you think they'll cancel school?"

Our driver leaned on his horn until the crowd parted and a way opened for us. He slowly piloted the bus to the curb and we unloaded.

Principal Gorton stood out front again playing traffic cop. She looked as if she was fending off mosquitoes. Whenever a car packed with sightseers tried to sneak through, she popped a silver whistle into her mouth and gave a sharp blast. She did not look like a happy camper.

"What a circus!" Gasser hooted as we tramped up the front walk between high banks of snow. He turned to take in the crowd. "Man, if we could charge admission, we'd make a mint."

We all cracked up.

All except Slingshot.

"Hold on now," he said. You could almost see the wheels turning in his head. "That's not a bad idea. Not a bad idea at all."

"What's not?" Stump laughed. "Getting steamrolled by a crazed mob?"

"I'm seeing a hot chocolate stand," said Slingshot. "All these people? In this cold? We'd make a fortune!"

We were quiet for a minute as Slingshot's idea sank in.

"In Florida we used to set up lemonade stands," ventured Orlando. "I've never heard of a hot chocolate stand."

"Same idea," said Slingshot. "Different weather."

"You know, it might just work," said Gabby. "Seriously. You think Principal Gorton would go for it?"

I glanced over at our intrepid leader. She made a series of hand gestures that looked like kung fu while fiercely tooting her whistle.

I didn't think she'd go for anything at the moment. Except maybe a big bottle of aspirin.

"Let's talk to Mr. Swickle," suggested Stump.

"C'mon! What've we got to lose?"

We funneled through the snow canyon into school. Without bothering to take off our coats, we surrounded Mr. Swickle and explained our idea.

"It's a once-in-a-lifetime opportunity!" Stump pleaded, hopping from foot to foot. He always bounced when he was excited. "When else will we ever have a crowd like this on our doorstep?!"

Mr. Swickle folded his arms across his chest. He was not convinced. Then I had an idea. "It could be a fund-raiser for charity," I ventured. "You know, a cool cause the whole school can support? Remember when we washed cars to raise money for the outfield wall at Rambletown Field? It'll be like that, except this time we donate the profits to something bigger!"

"That wall is pretty big," Orlando murmured, rubbing his head.

"You know what I mean," I said.

"Hmmm," Mr. Swickle said. "Community

service. I'll tell you what. Everybody take your seats. If we get through attendance without any problems, I'll make the necessary inquiries."

We didn't need to be asked twice.

We stowed our winter stuff and sat at our desks in no time flat. We folded our hands and beamed at Mr. Swickle like angels. After calling roll, he told us to get out our workbooks and copy down today's poem. Then he opened the door between our room and the other sixth-grade class next door and asked the teacher, Mrs. Nedermeyer, to keep an eye on us.

"I have to talk to Principal Gorton about something important," he explained. "I'll fill you in when I get back."

Without waiting for an answer, he dashed out of the room.

Through the open doorway, I saw Ducks and Ocho and the other guys settling in for class. Boy, would they be in for a surprise if we could pull off this thing.

★ CHAPTER 14 ★

The new poem was called "Watermelon." It was by a guy named Charles Simic. Mr. Swickle had written that Charles Simic was a poet laureate of the United States of America. I guessed that meant he was like the president of all the poets.

Thinking of presidents made me look outside. Our frozen four were still up there. The curious crowd, I noted with satisfaction, was still there too, and getting bigger.

The poem was really short. It was about watermelons. The poet thought they looked like fat little statues of the Buddha. When the fruit was cut open, the red wedges reminded him of smiles.

I thought a smile was a cool way to describe a watermelon because eating one made you happy.

Biting into a real watermelon would have been nice. It would have meant summer and hot weather and no more slushy boots and wet mittens. It would have meant no mitts at all, except the baseball kind.

I finished copying the poem, and Mr. Swickle still hadn't come back. The long red second hand on the big clock above the blackboard inched forward. In a race with a tortoise, it would have lost by a mile.

Finally, the hall door swung open, and Mr. Swickle walked briskly through the doorway. He nodded to Mrs. Nedermeyer. I tried to read his expression, but his face was like a crossword puzzle with no boxes filled in. It was blank.

"Well," he said after about a hundred years had passed. "Yes, indeed."

"Yes, what?" I wanted to shout.

"Principal Gorton has pressed the cafeteria

ladies into service. As we speak, Mr. Trombley and his men have begun setting up folding tables."

Mr. Trombley is the school custodian.

"The first ever Rambletown Elementary School hot chocolate stand is a go!"

Room 12 exploded in cheers. Through the open door, the kids in Mrs. Nedermeyer's class snapped their heads around and stared.

"Ahem," said Mr. Swickle. He turned to Mrs. Nedermeyer, who looked as curious as her students. "Sudden change of plans," he explained. "A fund-raiser to service the frozen hordes outside. The whole school will participate."

"When?" asked Mrs. Nedermeyer.

"Now." Mr. Swickle beamed.

An excited murmur broke out among her kids.

"I never got the memo," complained Mrs. Nedermeyer. "My lesson plan is all made up. We're ready for a big day of diagramming sentences. Definitive articles, noun markers, prepositional phrases."

Whispers turned to groans in her room.

"There was no memo," said Mr. Swickle brightly. "The kids just dreamed it up this morning. Principal Gorton agrees that we should seize the moment. Strike while the iron is hot. Carpe diem and all that."

"What about my definitive articles?" asked Mrs. Nedermeyer. "My beautiful noun markers?"

"They'll keep," said Mr. Swickle. "But the crowd outside may not."

We settled down and listened intently as Mr. Swickle explained how the fund-raiser would work. Five tables would be set up at different points around the parking lot, each with its own steaming vat of hot chocolate. Classes would take turns manning the tables. Everyone would have a job. Some kids would collect money from customers, some would fill cups, others would push carts loaded with fresh urns of hot chocolate from the cafeteria to the tables outside.

Best of all, since the whole thing was our idea, our class got to go first.

Slingshot raised his hand.

"Yes?" asked Mr. Swickle.

"How much are we charging?"

"A buck a cup. It's a nice round figure and will keep things simple. We won't have to make a lot of change."

The only thing left to decide was how to use the proceeds. Mr. Swickle asked if we had any ideas.

We had plenty.

Many of them had to do with new, cool stuff for the school. Like a swimming pool. With waterslides. And a sprinkler park.

"Why not some trained dolphins that could swim around the deep end doing tricks?" asked Mr. Swickle

I detected sarcasm.

"People, people," he said. "The idea is to use the money to help other people, remember?"

We got serious after that. Our class thought

of a million good causes, but Orlando came up with the best one of all. Maybe the fact that he came from Florida gave him the idea. Or maybe he simply glanced out the window at the shivering presidents.

In any case, his hand suddenly shot in the air.

"Go ahead, Orlando," Mr. Swickle said.

"Coats for Kids?" the center fielder suggested. "I read about it in the paper. It's a program to provide warm clothes to families who need them right here in town."

We talked it over. It was perfect.

"It's unanimous," Mr. Swickle said. "Coats for Kids."

At precisely 9:45, we donned our coats, pulled on our hats and gloves and boots, and followed Mr. Swickle outside.

I couldn't believe my eyes. In the last hour, every person in Rambletown apparently had gathered in the lot. Many had brought friends from out of town.

"That's a lot of cold people," Slingshot observed.

"Ka-ching!' exclaimed Stump.

We took up our posts. Gasser, Orlando, and I commanded a table near the main entrance to school. We were cashiers. Slingshot and Gabby waited at either end of the table, ready to fill paper coffee cups from big, brown, plastic urns. Stump and several other classmates stood on alert behind pushcarts, primed to race back to the cafeteria for fresh supplies of liquid warmth.

"Come and get it!" bellowed Gasser. "Fresh hot chocolate! Getcher hot chocolate here." His years of playing baseball obviously had not been wasted: He sounded exactly like a ballpark vendor.

Instantly, a swarm of noisy, red-nosed customers descended on us. They pressed dollar bills into our hands like money was litter they couldn't wait to toss. We replaced greenbacks with steaming cups. The money went into a tin box, the hot chocolate went down the hatch, and the customers—or so it seemed to me—went directly back to the end of the line to wait for seconds. You couldn't have made money faster if you had your own printing press.

An hour passed in no time flat. We were so busy, I didn't even feel the cold. At the end of our shift, Mrs. Nedermeyer's class arrived to replace us. I counted up our haul before handing over the tin box to Ocho.

"One hundred and thirty-four dollars!" I announced.

Slingshot quickly did the math. "One thirty-four times five tables is six hundred and seventy dollars," he said. "If we pull in that much every hour until school ends at two forty-five, we'll make three thousand three hundred and fifty dollars."

Slingshot is a whiz with numbers.

I didn't know how many coats you could get for kids who didn't have them with three thousand three hundred and fifty dollars. But I knew it was a lot. Despite the kooky cold weather, I suddenly felt very warm inside.

On the way back into school, I surveyed the wild scene and spotted Principal Gorton. She still waved her hands, but she'd given up blowing the whistle. Instead, she shouted, "Hot chocolate! Getcher hot chocolate here!"

For the first time since spring break ended, she looked happy.

★ CHAPTER 15 ★

The fund-raiser was a huge success.

Our attempt to practice at Rambletown Field Thursday afternoon was anything but. The lumpy mounds of snow ringing the diamond looked like a bunch of white camels. And the ground was so crusty and hard you could twist an ankle just by looking at it.

Even Skip Lou had to admit that pretending to play baseball in those conditions made less sense than change for a nickel. Shaking his head, Skip gathered us around for a quick conference.

"Listen up, guys," he started. "I hate to say it, but until this snow melts we're going to have to move inside. It won't be perfect, but anything's better than careening all over a giant slippery slide."

He was right about that. We all had the bumps and bruises to prove it. Especially Orlando.

"Let's head back to school and set up in the gym," Skip continued. "We can run some really fun drills on the basketball court. Glove and Tugboat, you guys grab the equipment bags. Everybody else, get your stuff and let's go."

We followed him off the diamond. Our breath puffed white in the wintry air as we chugged single file back to school. Banked snow squeezed the sidewalk, leaving a cleared path about as wide as a Habitrail. A hamster could have scooted along it with ease, if it was an extraskinny hamster.

Reaching school, we threaded past sight-seers ogling Mount Rambletown. I counted three TV news crews. The smiles on the report-ers' faces looked frozen in place as they gazed into their cameras. The gusting wind ruined their perfect hair. Between takes, they stamped their feet and hugged themselves for warmth. I felt bad that we had no hot chocolate for them today.

We trudged behind the school to the back entrance to the gym, where Skip unlocked the wide double doors and flipped on the lights one after another.

"You guys stow your coats and stuff on the bleachers," Skip directed. "I'll get a basket of training balls from the equipment room. Be lined up on the baseline under the basket when I get back."

Our wet boots squeaked on the shining wooden floor as we tramped across the basketball court. It sounded like a choir of songbirds. Real songbirds would have been nice. They would have meant spring had sprung.

"I'll bet you never played baseball on a hoops court in Florida," I said to Orlando as I yanked off my snow pants. Underneath, I wore a pair of gray sweats.

"Never," he agreed. "Then again, I never skidded into the outfield wall ten times in one day either."

Skip returned, rolling a wheeled basket of baseballs. Except they weren't real baseballs, I knew. They were lighter, made of some sort of soft, rubbery material that bounced harmlessly off walls and lights and human bodies. We'd used them in T-ball and Coaches Pitch when I was a kid. Skip pushed the cart to the sideline and walked onto the court.

Apparently we wouldn't be getting to the balls just yet.

"Let's start with some sprints," Skip said from the free throw line.

A groan went up from the team.

"Suicides?" Stump asked.

In the front row of bleachers, Gasser stretched out his broken leg and grinned. "Bummer! I do hate to miss this," he lied.

Skip Lou explained the rules. Probably he didn't need to. So-called suicide sprints were like black jelly beans. One taste and you never forgot how awful they were.

"I thought you said this would be fun," Ducks complained.

"Patience," Skip said. "Ready?"

I crouched low, my right hand touching the floor for balance. Skip blew his whistle and off we thundered like stampeding cattle.

The Glove took an early lead with Orlando running a close second. The Glove led us in stolen bases every season. It would be interesting to see if Orlando could stay with the fleet second baseman.

I reached the free throw line, slapped it, and changed directions. Ocho and Stump breathed down my neck as I darted back to the baseline. I tagged it and immediately turned again and raced to center court. By the time I got there, Orlando and the Glove had already passed me heading the other way, still neck and neck. On dry ground, Orlando clearly didn't have any trouble with speed.

"One to go," Skip shouted as we took off on the last leg, a brutal full-court sprint. "Dig! Dig! Dig!"

I made it to the far end of the court, turned, and kicked for home. I was still a short jump shot from finishing when Orlando and the Glove crossed the line dead even. I followed them in third, narrowly edging out Stump, Ocho, and the rest of the guys.

"Great wheels, everybody," said Skip Lou as we gasped for air. "With speed like that, we'll be terrors on the base paths this year. Grab some water and then we'll split up into teams for Wall Ball."

Orlando's head jerked up: "Wall Ball?" he asked.

"Don't worry," Gasser said with a laugh. "The idea is to hit a ball off the wall, not run into it. You'll be fine."

After a brief rest we formed two equal squads. Half of us, the Blues, grabbed our gloves and spread out along one end of the basketball court. The other half, the Reds, lined up at the opposite end, where Skip Lou had set up a batting tee. One at a time the Reds—Slingshot, Tugboat, Ducks, Ocho, and Kid Rabbit— whacked a ball off the tee. If it got past us and hit the wall, they scored a point.

Stump hoovered up a hot grounder. Gilly snared a liner in his big first baseman's mitt. I knocked down a dangerous flare, and the Glove made a nice backhanded stab on a tricky bounder.

But Orlando stole the show, leaping high to spear a rocket off the bat of Tugboat an inch in front of the gym's bruising cinder block wall. He landed cleanly on his feet and soft-tossed the ball back to Skip Lou, smiling as if to say he could make that play any day of the week.

As long as snow didn't cover the ground, I believed he could.

We played for a solid hour. At the end of it, the Reds had scored six times, and we had bounced seven hits off the wall. But the best number of all was zero. Which was the sum total of Orlando's collisions.

Practice broke up with all of us feeling a little better about our chances against the Haymakers. And a whole lot better about our new center fielder's prospects for survival.

CHAPTER 16

Snow fell heavily all night, and on Friday morning there was no question about school. It was like an old stamp: canceled.

Normally I would have been thrilled. Not much beats a snow day. But we'd already had so many that they were no better than yesterday's *Rambletown Bulletin*. They were old news. At this rate, we'd have so many makeup days, we'd still be going to school in July. Maybe it would have warmed up by then. I hoped so. I didn't want to be huddled under blankets to watch the Fourth of July fireworks.

I joined my mom and dad at the breakfast

table and poured myself a bowl of Pirate Crunch.

"You lucky duck," said Dad. "I wish I could take a snow day. Unfortunately, the office doesn't close."

"You're the lucky one," I said. "I'm sick of snow days. I'm sick of snow."

My dad nearly fell off his chair.

"Sick of snow days? Whoever heard of such a thing? It's blasphemy."

"Whoever heard of such a miserable winter?" I said. "If it doesn't let up, baseball season will never start."

"Good point," Dad said. He opened the morning paper and turned to the weather page. "Look here," he announced. "Changing to sunny by this afternoon. Tomorrow's supposed to be even warmer."

"See, honey," said Mom. "There's hope yet." She leaned across the table and lightly kissed my head. "I've got a good feeling. I think winter is on its last legs."

I looked out the window. A thick white blanket covered the lawn.

"I don't know about legs," I said skeptically. "Stilts maybe."

Real stilts would have been nice. We could have used them to walk over all that snow.

After breakfast I bundled into my Inuit parka, pulled on my ski hat and my down-filled mittens, and laced up my mukluks. Then I zipped Mr. Bones into his silly coat. We went out into the frosty morning and started shoveling the driveway. At least I did. Mr. Bones bounded around the yard poking his furry head under the snow in search of buried tennis balls.

It took me about an hour to clear a path down to the street. As I neared the end, Slingshot and Stump showed up. Slingshot wore a backpack. Stump carried a giant duffel bag. They had the look of foxes with keys to the henhouse.

"What's in the bags?" I asked.

"Top secret," said Stump.

"C'mon," said Slingshot. "Let's go."

"Go where?" I asked, leaning on my shovel. I couldn't tell if it was the work I'd done or the weather, but I actually felt warm. I unzipped my coat.

"School," said Stump.

"Maybe you haven't heard," I said. "School's canceled."

"All the better," said Slingshot, "to test my invention."

"What invention?" I asked.

"The one that's going to keep Orlando from running into the wall."

This sounded interesting. "Let me ask my mom," I said.

"We already did," Stump assured me. "Talked on the phone while you were shoveling. Everything's cool."

I turned and looked back at the house. Mom waved from a patch of sunlight on the porch. "Good luck," she called. I noticed she wasn't even wearing a coat. Maybe the paper was right. Maybe the weather was warming up at last.

With that the three of us rushed off, Mr. Bones scampering in our tracks.

All along the route to school, grown-ups cleared sidewalks and laughing kids built snowmen and snow forts. Sunlight glinted off the fresh white stuff, making the day blindingly bright. People smiled and waved and said things like "Enjoy it while you can."

In other words, a perfect winter scene.

Except it was April.

Obviously none of these people played baseball.

When we got to the school yard, we found Orlando and the rest of the Rounders pegging one another with snowballs. Gabby was there, camera slung around her neck as usual. A few tourists milled around the base of Mount Rambletown, but the crowd was much thinner than it had been earlier in the week.

Slingshot led us across the parking lot to the mountain. He shrugged off his pack and set it down in the snow.

"What's the idea?" I asked.

"The idea," said Slingshot, "is to give Orlando some traction."

"I like it," said Orlando. "But how?"

"With these," said Slingshot. He unzipped his pack and pulled out two sheets of sandpaper.

"What's he supposed to do with those?" I asked. "Rub splinters out of the outfield wall? The goal is to stop Orlando from hitting the wall. Not make his collisions smoother!"

"He'll need more than sandpaper for that," Ducks agreed.

With a shake of his head, Slingshot reached into his pack again. Out came a pair of shoes with spikes on the bottom.

"Those are golf shoes," said Tugboat.

"Borrowed from my dad," said Slingshot.

"Uh, Slingshot," piped up Ocho. "I hate to

remind you, but we've got a baseball game coming up. Do you think this is the best time for Orlando to learn golf?"

"No, no, I get it," said Orlando. "Golf spikes will bite into the crusty snow. I can dig in and stop from slipping. But I still don't get the sandpaper."

Slingshot smiled and pressed a sheet of the gritty paper over the spikes on one shoe, rough side showing.

"Extra gripping power," he said. "Like snow tires for your feet." He stuck the other sheet of sandpaper on to the other shoe and handed the pair to Orlando. "Try them on," he said. "I stuffed newspaper in the toes so they'll fit better."

Orlando sat down in the snow and pulled off his boots. He laced up the golf shoes.

"Not bad," he said, standing. He shuffled his feet. The shoes scratched loudly, like a cat sharpening its claws. "They really grip," he said.

"Good!" said Slingshot. "Then let's get

started. To the summit!"

Orlando craned his neck and gazed up the steep slope of Mount Rambletown. "You want me to climb that thing?" he asked uncertainly.

"Name a better place to test the shoes," Slingshot said. "If they work here, they'll work anywhere. Including Rambletown Field."

"When you get to the top"—Stump grinned, reaching into his duffel—"plant this in the snow." He whipped out what looked like the world's largest roll of aluminum foil. Slingshot took one end and helped Stump unfurl it. The shimmering silver material opened up to the size of King Kong's bedsheet. Stitched to it in big block letters cut out of red felt were the words GO ROUNDERS! BEAT HOG CITY!

At that we all cheered like crazy.

"We made it out of a special kind of foil called Mylar," Stump said proudly. "Slingshot's idea. Lightweight and completely weatherproof."

"And big enough to see from halfway across the state," added Slingshot.

We were still clapping and chanting "Go Rounders, Go!" as Orlando started his ascent.

★ CHAPTER 17 ★

Slowly, carefully, Orlando tested the sticking power of Slingshot's sandpaper golf shoes. He stomped down one foot to dig the spikes into the snow. Then he stomped down the other. The shoes held, and he took another cautious half step up the steep mountain. Each time he repeated the process, his confidence built and he increased his pace. Soon he was really chugging along, his movements crisp and machinelike.

"That's the way, Orlando!" I hollered. "Steady as she goes!"

Up and up he climbed, like a fly walking straight up a wall. The higher he went, the smaller he got. Before long, we could make out nothing more than his red hat bobbing ever upward against a solid white background. Then Orlando disappeared altogether. We watched from way down below, our hearts pounding. All we could hear was the rush of wind across the jagged peak.

I glanced at Slingshot and saw his face turn whiter than the snow. I knew that he'd never forgive himself if something went wrong.

None of us would.

We held our breaths. Time seemed to stand still. Suddenly the hat reappeared higher up the slope, still moving, still gaining.

"He's going to make it!" roared Ocho. "The kid from Florida is going to conquer this frozen wonder of the world!"

The color returned to Slingshot's face.

We smacked high fives and bumped chests. We jumped up and down as if the ground was made of rubber. Mr. Bones ran around, licking faces wherever he could reach them. None of us could stop shouting. I felt happier than the day we'd won the pennant.

Orlando reached the huddled presidents and did not pause. He scaled the bridge of FDR's nose and pulled himself to his full height atop the old guy's enormous head.

We cheered like crazy, and then roared even louder as he unfurled the huge, shimmering banner at the very summit of Mount Rambletown. Even at that great distance, its enormous red letters stood out boldly:

GO ROUNDERS! BEAT HOG CITY!

"He did it." Slingshot laughed. "He really did it!"

"A million small steps for a Rounder, one giant leap for Rounderkind," Stump crowed.

"Giant leap is right!" said Tugboat. "The outfield will be a cakewalk after this. I can't wait to see the look on Flicker Pringle's face the first time Orlando runs down one of his long balls at the wall. The Haymakers don't stand a chance!"

The silver banner caught the afternoon sun and glowed like a lighthouse. Tugboat slipped on a pair of shades. "Cool," he marveled. "It's like a giant solar reflector."

"We hoped it would be a real attention getter." Stump giggled.

"I think it's actually magnifying the sun's rays," said Gabby. "All of a sudden I feel warmer."

She had a point. My own head baked under my wool hat. If the warmth held, we might actually get to play our season opener after all. I wondered if Orlando felt the heat up at the shining summit.

If so, it didn't slow him down any. We watched him drop from Calvin Coolidge's left ear on to the president's shoulder. From there he edged under Silent Cal's chin and into a chute formed by his necktie. Orlando eased himself into it, pulled his knees up under his chin, and rocketed down Mount Rambletown like a turtle using its shell as a toboggan.

For a kid who'd never been sledding before, he was fantastic.

In no time flat he arrived at the base, nose red, eyes watering, mouth frozen in a smile wider than the Grand Canyon.

We gave him a hero's welcome. In fact, we carried him all the way home on our shoulders. His feet didn't touch the ground until we deposited him on his front doorstep.

We turned and looked toward school, where we caught the rays of the lowering sun glinting madly off the team banner atop Mount Rambletown. With one last cheer we said our good-byes, promising one another we'd all get a good night's sleep before the big game the next day.

★ CHAPTER 18 ★

I don't know about the other guys, but I broke my promise. I broke it like Ted Williams broke hitting records. I shattered it.

Lying in bed Friday night, I couldn't sleep at all. Despite Orlando's heroic climb, I still felt nervous. Butterflies played musical chairs in my stomach. It was thinking about the Hog City Haymakers that did it.

We had beaten them to win the championship last year. But that was then, as Flicker said, and this was now.

This was a new season. A new, cold, snowy season that was supposed to be spring but looked and felt an awful lot like winter.

This was a frozen field and cold bats that

stung your hands like swarms of bees and a center fielder who ran into walls.

This was the Hog City Haymakers out for vengeance. A team that would stop at nothing to get back the championship they thought they owned and we had stolen.

This was Flicker Pringle, the biggest, meanest Haymaker of them all. The kid with the best fastball anyone had ever seen. Or not. It moved so fast you couldn't.

The butterflies in my stomach started turning cartwheels. They did leaps and flips and forward rolls. It was regular butterfly gymnastics down there.

There's only one thing for butterfly gymnastics.

Fried baloney sandwiches.

I tossed aside the covers and rolled out of bed. Mr. Bones followed closely on my heels as I slipped downstairs. In the darkness of the kitchen, I started sizzling up baloney and toasting bread.

Mr. Bones sat down beside me and gazed

longingly at the smoking pan. The baloney hissed and popped. When the first batch was done, I shoveled it onto the bread and filled the pan again. Mr. Bones began to drool. The toaster ejected four more slices of bread, and I loaded them up with hot baloney.

I was so busy I didn't hear my dad slip into the kitchen.

"Ahem." He cleared his throat.

"Oh, hi," I said. "Hungry?"

He looked at me. He looked at the pan on the stove. He looked at the stack of sandwiches on the plate. He looked at the clock on the wall.

"You're cooking," he said, rubbing sleep from his eyes. "I thought the furnace was acting up. The whole house is full of smoke. Do you know what time it is?"

"Sorry," I said. "I couldn't sleep."

"Worried about the game?" he asked.

I nodded.

"As far as I know, you guys are still the

champs. You beat the Haymakers last year, remember? They're the ones who should be concerned."

I flipped the last sandwich onto the stack and clicked off the stove.

"Last year we didn't have a center fielder who ran into walls," I said, carrying the feast to the table. "If Orlando's new shoes don't work, he's going to knock himself goofy. And probably cost us the home opener."

"New shoes?" Dad asked.

"Long story," I said, reaching for a fried baloney sandwich. "You want one?"

"You go ahead," Dad said. "Eat."

Eat I did. So did Mr. Bones. A fried baloney sandwich for me, a fried baloney sandwich for Mr. Bones. Then another one for me and another one for him.

We ate our way clean through a pound of baloney and a whole loaf of old Leadbelly Sinker Bread.

The sandwiches did their trick. By the time I

finished eating, I was too stuffed to worry about much of anything. Except maybe popping the buttons on my pajamas.

"Now get some sleep," Dad said. "You still have a game tomorrow, you know."

"Don't remind me," I said. "That's what got me going in the first place."

I lumbered back upstairs and heaved myself into bed. Mr. Bones jumped up there with me and curled into a ball at my feet.

For the rest of the night, my room was like a forest. I slept like a log, and Mr. Bones slept like a rock.

★ CHAPTER 19 ★

When I next opened my eyes, a bright yellow glow filled the room. I sat up and blinked. I felt as if I was trapped inside a lemon.

I slid to the floor and ran to the window. I was psyched to see that no snow had fallen overnight. Even better, what remained from previous storms was melting fast. The bright yellow glow that filled my room was sunshine.

"Wake up," I called excitedly to Mr. Bones. "Spring is finally here."

He cocked his head and pricked his ears.

"That's right, you old furball," I teased. "It's curtains for that coat of yours."

I threw open the window and stuck out my head. The air carried the smell of the world waking up after a long nap. Warm and moist and earthy. I inhaled deeply. Someone should capture that scent and put it in a bottle. They'd make a million dollars selling it to people who were sick and tired of winter.

Dad was cooking up a storm when I came downstairs.

Omelets, of course.

"One Star-Spangled Special coming right up," he hollered over the roar of the CD player. "There's hits in omelets, you know!" The speakers pumped out "We Are the Champions" at earsplitting volume. Another game-day ritual of my dad's.

"Great!" I yelled back.

In truth, I wasn't all that hungry. Given all the fried baloney sandwiches I'd wolfed down the night before, I probably could've gotten by with a bowl of thin gruel. Whatever gruel is. But tradition is tradition. You don't mess with it.

Mom breezed in with a big smile on her face.

"Game on!" she shouted across the table. "Are you ready to rock those Haymakers?"

"You bet," I said.

"Hold on!" Mom shouted. She got up and lowered the volume on the music. "I can't hear myself think."

Dad frowned but didn't protest. The omelet had reached a delicate stage and required his full attention.

Mom unfolded the morning paper.

"Will you look at that?" she said.

Splashed across the front page was one of Gabby's pictures. It showed Mount Ramble-town with the team banner flying above the presidents. Clearly they were Rounders' fans.

The caption said:

Opening Day is finally here. It must be. What other explanation could there be for the enormous sign that mysteriously appeared atop Mount Rambletown yesterday? Here's hoping our hometown heroes reach the same dizzying heights as whatever brave soul planted it! Go, Rounders! Beat the Haymakers!

"Now, how do you suppose that got up there?" Mom wondered aloud.

"Beats me," I said.

"Breakfast is served," announced Dad, lumbering toward us under the enormous weight of a flying saucer–sized omelet. "Red, white, and blue in honor of the national pastime!"

Wagging his tail furiously, Mr. Bones parked himself beside my chair.

Dad set down the platter on the table. His creation was blue with ribbons of red pepper slices and white stripes of cheese. It looked like an American flag with the stars and stripes jumbled together.

"I'm afraid to ask," I said. I'd never seen blue eggs before.

"Blueberries," Dad said proudly. "Good and good for you."

Mr. Bones growled. "Enough with the questions," he seemed to say. "Let's eat!" Blue eggs didn't bother him one bit.

I cut off a corner of the scrambled flag and nibbled the edge. Not bad. Not bad at all. Quite good, in fact. I slipped Mr. Bones a piece under the table. He gulped it down and sat up for more.

"Can we give you a ride to the game?" Mom asked between bites.

"No thanks," I said. "Better stick to the routine." I always biked to home games. Of course, there'd never been snow on the ground before. But still. I didn't want to go changing things at the last minute.

"The plows were out yesterday, so the streets should be pretty clear," I said. "Plus, everything is melting fast."

"Okay then." Mom nodded. "We'll see you in the second inning."

This was another of our traditions. Mom and Dad came to all my games, but they always came late. It's a long story. Years ago they had missed the first inning by accident, and I ended up having the best game of my life. Hit about a gazillion dingers. Ever since then, they timed things so they arrived at the ballpark for the top of the second. Call it superstition, but it seemed to work.

I hoped it would today.

I scarfed down some stars and stripes and then dressed for the game. Winter coat over my uniform. That was a first. Then Mr. Bones and I headed over to the ballpark. Out of habit, I took my shovel.

The first thing I noticed when we got there was that the whole place shimmered. The air itself seemed to glow.

The second thing I noticed was snow. More precisely, the lack of it. Huge mounds still dotted the foul areas in the shadows of the stands, but the field itself was clear enough for baseball. The sudden thaw made things wet. Really wet. But the snow was gone.

Finally.

"I guess I won't need this after all," I said, ditching my shovel by the dugout.

"And it looks like I won't need any of these," said Orlando, coming up behind me. He wore the modified golf spikes on his feet.

He held a big cardboard box. A pair of old-fashioned wooden snowshoes stuck out the top. They looked like tennis rackets for feet. Many other pairs of shoes were crammed inside. Rubber galoshes. Tennis sneakers. Football cleats. Swim flippers. Ski boots. Even a pair of ice skates.

"I brought everything," Orlando explained. "Just in case."

"The sandpaper shoes are all you need," I said. "They really work. Just not in the way we expected."

Orlando glanced at his feet. "What are you talking about?" he asked.

"Check it out," I said. I pointed toward the summit of Mount Rambletown, visible above the naked tree line. Orlando shaded his eyes and looked to the sky.

He did a double take.

I didn't blame him. There seemed to be two suns up there. The regular one and a second one parked atop the mountain.

"The gigantic foil Ramblers sign," I explained. "It's acting like a huge mirror, reflecting the sun's rays right down onto the field. That's why everything's glowing so weirdly."

The sign also explained how so much snow had disappeared so quickly. The thing melted it like a laser beam.

"Whoa!" murmured Orlando. "Do you think it will last?"

I really had no idea.

"As long as the sun keeps shining," I said, "it should."

"It kind of makes me feel like a hamburger or something."

"Just make sure you put a lot of mustard on your relay throws," I joked.

By now the other guys had showed up and were marveling at the condition of the field.

"Sloppy but playable," said Tugboat, strapping on his catcher's gear. "Bring on the Haymakers!"

He hunkered down behind the plate, and the rest of us tossed our coats into the dugout and trotted out to the diamond to get loose. In all the glittery sunlight, warming up was like tightening a belt. It was a cinch.

As we tossed the ball around the infield, fans began filling the bleachers. Most were decked out in Rounders' red and white. Many carried thick blankets, as if they didn't trust the weather to stay warm. All wore sunglasses.

At a quarter till noon, Skip Lou called us into the dugout.

"I don't know how that ray gun of a banner got up on Mount Rambletown," he said. "And

I'm not sure I want to know. But I do know I'm ready for this game. I hope you guys are too!"

"We are!" we yelled in response.

"Good. Then let's play hard and play fair and have a good time out there."

No sooner had he finished his pep talk than the public-address system boomed to life. "And now," bellowed the announcer, "please welcome the reigning division champs, our very own Rambletown Rounders!"

We charged out of our dugout to a standing ovation. Packed shoulder to shoulder in the bleachers, fans stamped and cheered and screamed our names. After the longest winter on record, they were as eager to watch baseball as we were to play it. It felt great to be standing at third base wearing a Rounders uniform instead of a down-filled parka.

Over on the visitors' bench the Haymakers looked like a bunch of skinned knees. Sore. They scowled at us and spit wads of chewed-up sunflower seeds on the ground. But at least they didn't fire any snowballs.

The umpire gathered himself behind home plate.

"PLAY BALL!" he roared.

★ CHAPTER 20 ★

The first Haymaker splashed to the plate. He was enormous. All the Haymakers were big, but this guy was downright scary. He was built like a refrigerator with arms and legs. He stepped into the box and cocked his bat. The barrel twitched like a tiger's tail.

Slingshot wound up and delivered the first pitch of the game. Fastball on the inside corner.

"STRIKE ONE!" boomed the umpire.

The gargantuan batter spit a wad of chewed-up sunflower seeds. He looked at strike two, then coolly lashed Slingshot's third pitch past Gilly at first. As the ball skidded into a puddle in the right field corner, the Haymaker tagged first and chugged for second. Ocho snatched the ball out of the drink and rifled it in. The Haymaker slid into the bag, splashing mud all over the Glove.

When the tidal wave subsided, the umpire made his call.

"SAFE!" he roared.

"No worries," I chattered. "Get the next guy, Slingshot!"

Slingshot bore down. He struck out batter number two on four pitches. He got the one after that on a pop fly to Ducks Bunion in left. The runner on second feinted toward third but retreated to the bag as Ducks fired the ball in to me.

"Two down," I shouted. "Let's go, guys. Play is at first."

Then it was Flicker Pringle's turn to hit. Out in the bleachers, fans nervously adjusted their sunglasses. They knew. We all knew. If there is one thing Flicker Pringle can do even better than throw a baseball, it is hit a baseball.

"C'mon now, Slingshot," called Stump. "Strike him out! He's got nothing!"

Flicker snorted. "Nothing but power to any field," he growled. The eye black smeared under his eyes to block the white glare reflecting down from atop Mount Rambletown looked like war paint. He crowded the plate, stirring the air with his bat.

Slingshot hurled some high cheese.

A lesser hitter would have swung right under the speeding ball. Not Flicker. He smashed it into deep center field. The second he connected, he dropped his bat and triumphantly raised both arms in the air.

In center field, Orlando turned and galloped toward the deepest part of the park. Mud splashed up at every step he took.

Orlando would have caught the ball, too.

Except for one thing.

He ran out of room.

"Look out!" I yelled from third base.

The fans in the bleachers saw what was about to happen and sucked in their breath all at

once. They'd read Gabby's report. They understood Orlando's wall problem. The noise they
made was the sound of all the air going right
out of the stadium. For a second, Rambletown
Field was perfectly quiet. Then a fearsome
crash shattered the uneasy calm.

Sha-bam!

Orlando rammed into the wall like a bull-
dozer.

As he tumbled to the ground, the ball sailed
right over him. It landed in the bleachers for a
homer.

Flicker dragged out his glory forever.
Magellan circled the globe in less time than it
took Flicker to round the bases. When he finally
made it home, he jumped on the plate with both
feet.

Slingshot glowered at the showboating pitcher from high atop the mound. But all the hard
looks in the world couldn't change the score.

Just like that, the Haymakers led two to
nothing.

"Time!" called Skip Lou. He clattered up the

dugout steps and picked his way between puddles to center field.

The rest of the infielders and I trotted behind. By the time we got to Orlando, he was up and talking to fellow outfielders Ocho and Ducks.

"Are you all right, kid?" Skip asked. "That looked like a doozy."

"It's nothing," said Orlando. "The only thing that hurts is the homer. I thought I had it."

"Forget the homer," said Skip. "You've got to stop beating up on that wall. See all these people out here?"

Orlando glanced at the bleachers and nodded.

"Well, son, they came to watch a baseball game. Not a demolition derby. Promise me, no more ramming the wall."

"I promise, Skip," Orlando said sheepishly.

Skip Lou patted him on the back. "Good. Now, let's get out of this inning!"

"Yeah!" we all shouted.

"PLAY BALL!" roared the umpire once we were all in position again.

Slingshot wound up and delivered a sneaky curveball. The Haymaker batter lunged awkwardly at it, sending a dribbler back toward the mound. As wet as the field was, it really did dribble, too. Slingshot swooped down on the sodden ball like an owl catching dinner and fired to Gilly for out number three.

Ducks led off for us and saw three straight Flicker fastballs.

Only he didn't see them.

They zipped past him way too fast.

"STRIKE ONE!" hollered the ump.

"STRIKE TWO!"

"STRIKE THREE, YOU'RE OUT!"

Ducks trudged back to the bench, and Stump took his place in the batter's box. Different batter, same story. Rolling his trademark toothpick around in his mouth, Flicker whiffed him on a trio of invisible heaters.

Then it was my turn.

Billy Wishes handed me my favorite Louisville Slugger.

"Wallop one to Kalamazoo," he said.

"I'll sure try," I said, rubbing the batboy's head for luck.

Under the blinding double sun, I dug in at the plate, determined to get our first hit of the game.

In the stands, fans stood and chanted my name. They still remembered my walk-off homer in the championship game, I guessed. I scanned the crowd for my parents and saw two empty places where they usually sat. It boosted my confidence to know they were sticking with tradition. Fired up, I locked into my stance.

Flicker reared back and gunned a handful of smoke in my direction.

I heard the ball, but I didn't see it.

It whooshed like a bottle rocket, then exploded with a pop.

The pop was the ball slamming into the catcher's mitt.

After that came a telltale "Yowch!"

The "Yowch" came from the catcher. It hurt to catch Flicker's sizzling fastballs.

After the catcher, it was the ump's turn to speak up.

"STRIKE ONE!" he roared.

Flicker rolled his toothpick. That made me mad. I knew it was his way of laughing. He reached back and served up a second helping of fastball.

Whoosh! Pop! "Yowch!"

Strike two left as bad a taste in my mouth as the first one.

"Come on now, kid," Skip Lou called from the bench. "It only takes one. Look for your pitch."

"He can look all he wants," sneered Flicker. "He still won't see nothing."

I clapped down my helmet and made like a frozen can of orange juice. I concentrated. Flicker wound up and launched a rocket. I swung.

Crack!

I knew the ball was gone the second it left my bat. The only question was if it would be fair.

Fans jumped to their feet and roared. Blowing a kiss to the left field foul pole as it breezed past, the ball dropped into the bleachers.

"FAIR BALL!" bleated the ump.

I rounded the bases calmly and quickly, as if homering off Flicker Pringle was no big deal. But inside I was like a bike tire. I was pumped.

Tugboat came up after me and grounded out to short to end the inning.

We went to the second down a run but right back in it.

★ CHAPTER 21 ★

Slingshot kept the Haymakers off the bases in the second. When it was Flicker's turn in the bottom half of the inning, he did too. He threw darts, BBs, bullets, missiles. We swung gamely; but as hard as he threw, we would have had more success trapping wind in a butterfly net.

Hog City added a run in the top of the third on a string of squib hits. In the bottom half, we caught a break when Ocho and the Glove reached base on back-to-back infield errors. With no outs, it looked like we stood a pretty good chance of bringing in the tying run, maybe even taking the lead.

Flicker Pringle quickly laid our hopes to rest by fanning Ducks, Stump, and me one after another.

Midway through the game, the Haymakers' 3–1 lead was holding up better than their catchers. Flicker wore these guys out like old blue jeans. They couldn't take more than an inning of his heat. The used-up ones sat side by side in the dugout, their swollen hands buried in tubs of ice.

Flicker didn't care. He kept firing away. And we kept swinging.

And missing.

Slingshot pitched a one-two-three fourth inning. Flicker Pringle matched him pitch for pitch, striking out Tugboat, Orlando, and Gilly.

As we took the field for the fifth, shadows began to creep like doubt across the field. With the sun dipping toward the horizon, the afternoon turned as cold as our bats had been all day. Suddenly, it felt like winter again.

Fortunately, the Haymakers were ice-cold

too. They managed no hits in the fifth.

Slingshot led off for us in the bottom half and swung for all he was worth at Flicker's first pitch. Maybe Flicker was tiring. Or maybe Slingshot actually saw the ball for once now that the glare from atop Mount Rambletown had died. Or it could have been nothing more than good hitting. Whatever the reason, Slingshot actually struck the ball. In the dugout, we jumped up and roared.

It was our first hit of the game since my homer way back in the top frame.

At least it would've been our first hit. If the ball had actually gone anywhere. It didn't. Instead, it just disintegrated. Vanished in a puff of powder. Poof. It was gone.

I'd never seen anything like it.

"FOUL BALL!" cried the umpire.

Slingshot shook his head like a fisherman who'd let one get away. He dug in again. Flicker whipped another bullet.

Whoosh! went the pitch.

Swish! went the swing.

Poof! went the ball.

"FOUL!" roared the umpire as the ball vaporized in a fine mist. "STRIKE TWO!"

"If that don't beat all," said Skip Lou.

Slingshot stepped back and tucked his bat under his arm. He clapped his hands in frustration. When he stood back in, Flicker popped off another fastball.

Whoosh!

Swish!

Poof!

The ball vanished in thin air.

Again.

"FOUL BALL!" roared the umpire.

Before Flicker could throw another pitch, Billy Wishes charged out of the dugout and on to the diamond.

I wondered if maybe he was looking for his marbles. He seemed to have lost them.

"Get back here, Billy," Skip called after him. "You can't run on the field in the middle of a game!"

Billy kept going.

"No fair!" he shouted, rushing the mound. "He's throwing slush balls! That's why Slingshot can't hit them! Flicker Pringle's packing slush balls! He grabbed a big wad from the heap by the dugout between innings. I saw him!"

All of a sudden it got very quiet at Rambletown Field. Every person in the ballpark turned and looked toward the mound. Sure enough, Flicker Pringle was furiously dumping snow out of his oversized pitcher's mitt.

"Way to go, Billy," I screamed. "Great eyes, kid! I don't know how the rest of us missed it."

The umpire trotted out to the mound, raising his mask as he ran. He took one look at the big wet spot on Flicker's glove where he'd been hiding the snow and jabbed his thumb over his shoulder.

"YOU'RE OUT OF HERE!" he bellowed.

Snarling like a mountain lion, Flicker stamped off the mound. He was furious, but he had no case. He'd been caught red-handed. More accurately, he'd been caught blue-handed from packing wet snow. Why he wanted to do that, I'll never know. It wasn't as if he needed an edge. With an official baseball, he was already pitching a one-hitter.

In any case, he had to leave the game. There was no reason to believe any of his teammates were cheating, so the Haymakers were allowed to finish the game. But they were forced to send in a substitute pitcher.

It was thanks to Flicker Pringle's mean-spiritedness that our luck began to change.

Unfortunately, the weather continued to change right along with it.

Thick clouds rolled in from the north and blocked out the sun as completely as if someone had drawn the blinds. With no sunlight left to reflect, the banner atop Mount Rambletown was snuffed out like a candle in a hurricane. The temperature instantly plunged. In the stands, fans broke out their blankets. All over the field, puddles of melted snow began to freeze. The footing turned from sloppy to downright treacherous.

Slingshot took a curve for strike one from the new Haymaker hurler, Dirty Joe Dartoe, then tagged the next pitch. This time the ball did not explode. It bounced squarely between short and third for a hit. Ocho followed with a blooper into short right. The fielder charged in and slipped on a patch of new ice. By the time he came up with the ball, Ocho stood on second and Slingshot occupied third.

The Glove came up next. Swinging on the first pitch, he smashed a drive into left field. For a moment it looked like it would carry to the wall. A gust of wind knocked it down, however, and the left fielder squeezed the ball for our first out of the inning. The runners did not advance. Tugboat followed with a pop-up to first for out number two. Then Stump beat out a crafty bunt to keep our rally alive.

With two outs and the bases loaded, I came up to bat.

I'd knocked a hit off Flicker Pringle; I

meant to get one off the new guy, too.

A long one.

I took my bat from Billy, rubbing his head for luck. As I made my way to the plate, a pair of bright orange objects out in the bleachers caught my eye. I did a double take. It was Principal Gorton, waving her gloved hands in the air. Next to her sat Mr. Swickle. A group of kids in new winter coats filled the row in front of them. A few seats away, my mom and dad stood and waved. I smiled and tipped my helmet before settling in to hit.

The pitcher whipped a fastball. Compared to a Flicker Pringle fastball, it moved like frozen molasses. I practically had time to read a book.

I swung the bat and walloped the ball clear into the bleachers, where Principal Gorton caught it in her orange traffic mitts.

Grand slam!

Slingshot scored. Ocho cruised home right behind him, followed closely by Stump. Then I crossed the plate with our fifth run of the game.

The Haymakers still had only three.

Tugboat came up after me and went down quietly on strikes. Our side was retired. But we had taken the lead. We were only three outs away from a season-opening win.

★ CHAPTER 22 ★

As we jogged out to start the sixth and final frame, an icy wind howled through the ballpark. Dragon-shaped clouds filled the sky. Real dragons would have been nice. They breathe fire, and fire is warm. With the sudden deep-freeze, the field now looked like some kind of fancy dessert. It had more frosting than a birthday cake.

Slingshot wound up and let fly.

The huge Haymaker batter jumped all over the pitch, ripping a grounder toward second base. The Glove lunged, but his feet flew out from under him. As he hurtled across the icy ground on his back, the ball squirted away.

Stump pounced on it and gunned it to Gilly at first.

"SAFE!" called the umpire.

The next batter worked the count full before Slingshot buckled his knees with a nasty curveball for strike three.

Luck smiled on us when, with one out, the next hitter scorched a liner straight to center. For the first time since I'd known him, Orlando didn't have to move an inch to make the catch. It settled into his mitt like a pigeon coming home to roost. He flung the ball back in to the Glove, then waved his arm in the air.

"Time!" he hollered.

The umpire stepped from behind the plate and removed his mask.

"What is it, son?"

"I'm stuck," Orlando yelled. "I can't move."

The Haymakers roared with laughter.

The ump waved to Skip Lou on the bench. "Better see what this is about," he said.

Skip Lou jogged carefully to center, weaving

around the larger ice patches. I followed him out from third while Ocho and Ducks trotted over from their sides of the outfield.

"It's the shoes," Orlando whispered as we gathered around him. He was standing in the middle of a patch of ice the size of a hockey rink. "The spikes sunk into the mud. But it's gotten so cold, so fast, the ground froze around them while I stood here. It's like I'm nailed into concrete."

"Quick," Skip Lou ordered. "Unlace those crazy things and run to the dugout for a change. You did bring an extra pair, didn't you?"

"Oh, I brought other shoes all right," Orlando said.

He unlaced his sandpaper spikes and sprinted to the bench in his socks. Our fans cheered him every cold step of the way. Not the Haymakers, though. They pointed and jeered.

Ducks, Ocho, and I worked on freeing the modified golf spikes. After a good bit of wrangling, we managed to pry them loose. I handed them to Skip, who raised them in the air to more cheers from the crowd.

"Well, boys," he said with a shake of his head. "I have now officially seen everything. I'll tell you what. Let's end this game before anything else crazy happens." He trotted back to the bench, and I ran in to third.

Orlando passed me going the other way. He seemed to have gotten taller. He was also walking funny. Kind of wobbly at the ankles. He reached the big frozen pond of center field and began to glide. Then I saw what was different. The kid from Florida had swapped his spikes for a pair of ice skates.

Everyone else saw what he was up to at the same time.

"This isn't hockey," hooted the Haymakers. "This is baseball!"

Orlando paid no attention. Sweeping into position with a textbook hockey stop, he sprayed a fountain of shaved ice from his silver blades.

The crowd roared its approval. He was a good skater.

The Haymakers manager didn't like it one bit. He charged out to the plate and thrust his face in the ump's. His jaw pumped like a nutcracker's as he complained bitterly about Orlando's choice of footwear.

After listening politely for a few seconds, the ump threw his hands in the air.

"There's nothing in the rule book about skates," he said. "I guess he can wear them if he wants. Let's just finish this crazy game."

The manager reluctantly returned to the dugout. The Haymakers booed.

"BATTER UP!" roared the umpire.

Slingshot checked the runner on first, then snapped off a curve. The batter got a piece of it, rolling a slow one back up the middle. The ball squibbed over the mound, eluding Slingshot. Stump charged in, lost his footing, and flopped on his face. The ball hopped into short left field, where Ducks scooped it up and fired to me covering the bag at third.

I caught his throw and swept my glove toward the sliding runner.

"SAFE!" shouted the umpire.

With two outs, the Haymakers had runners on second and third. One hit would likely tie the game. A homer would put the Haymakers ahead. We had to stop them. But how could we? We were tumbling like dice out there.

Flicker Pringle's substitute stepped up to the plate for his first at bat of the game. If he was nervous, he sure didn't show it. He wiped his mustache on his sleeve. It was a big handlebar job. It made him look like a walrus, if walruses could swing bats the size of telephone poles.

The runner on second edged toward third. The runner on third sneaked toward home.

Slingshot grooved a greasy slider. The batter swung. Crack! The ball rose from his bat like an eagle.

Deep center field!

Back!

Way back!

Orlando put down his head and skated.

He went faster and faster. The ball flew farther and farther. The wall came closer and closer.

"Look out, Orlando!" I yelled.

He barreled straight for the high, hard center field wall. The exact same spot he'd crashed into so many times before.

Orlando didn't hear me. If he did, he didn't listen. He poured on speed until he was rattling across the ice like a human bobsled. I swear sparks flew out from under his skate blades.

The ball and Orlando arrived at the wall at the same time. Orlando leaped.

"Ooooh!" groaned a thousand Rounders fans in unison, expecting the worst.

One runner crossed the plate. Two runners crossed the plate.

The entire Hog City team raced out of the visitors' dugout and jumped up and down on the plate. Leading the celebration was Flicker Pringle.

As he flew through the air in center, Orlando reached up with his glove. The ball disappeared. Orlando's momentum carried him into the wall. Only this time he didn't bounce off it.

He hit it feetfirst and stuck.

The toes of his skates bit into the wood like arrows shot from a bow. Suspended three feet above the ground with his back toward home, he reached into his mitt. Like a rabbit coming out of a magician's hat, the baseball appeared in his hand. Orlando waved it over his head for all to see.

"YOU'RE OUT!" boomed the umpire. "GAME OVER!"

"NO WAY!" screamed Flicker. "HE CHEATED! HE USED HIS SKATES TO CLIMB THE WALL!"

"He made the catch before he stuck to the wall," ruled the ump. "Fair catch. Game over. Besides, didn't I already toss you?"

Flicker stomped off.

"ROUNDERS WIN! ROUNDERS WIN! ROUNDERS WIN!" yelled the announcer again and again as fans went bonkers.

Gasser led the charge from the bench. Working his crutches like ski poles, he raced out to Orlando. The whole team ran slip-sliding into the outfield behind him. Mr. Bones dashed along with us. He got to Orlando first and tried to climb the wall to lick his face.

Orlando reached down and scratched Mr. Bones behind the ears.

"I got it," panted Gasser.

"No, you don't," said Gilly. "You don't have it at all. Orlando does. He made the catch that won the game."

"The greatest catch ever!" added Tugboat. "Way to go, bro!"

"No," insisted Gasser, balancing on one leg as he waved his crutches in the air. "I've got it! I've got Orlando's nickname! Velcro! Orlando "Velcro" Ramirez. He's a superstar center fielder who catches the ball and sticks to the wall like Velcro."

"Word," said Ocho.

For about half a second, we thought it over. Then we pried our center fielder off the wall and carried him from the field on our shoulders. At that moment his smile was the biggest thing in the entire city. Not even Mount Rambletown with its bizarre, flag-waving presidents topped it. The only thing that came close was the din of the frenzied crowd, a thousand voices strong, as it screamed deliriously for Orlando "Velcro" Ramirez, the center fielder who stuck to walls.

Which was altogether better than running smack into them.

RAMBLETOWN ROUNDERS LINEUP
FOR THE SEASON OPENER
AGAINST HOG CITY HAYMAKERS

(with batting averages from the previous season)

PLAYER	POSITION	THROWS	BATS	BA
Ducks Bunion	left field	left	left	.301
Stump Plumwhiff	shortstop	right	right	.280
The Great Walloper Banjo H. Bishbash	third base	right	right	.560
Tugboat Tooley	catcher	right	right	.277
Orlando Ramirez	center field	left	left	.326[*]
Gilly Wishes	first base	left	left	.309
Slingshot Slocum	pitcher	right	right	.333
Octavio "Ocho" James	right field	right	right	.286
Ellis "the Glove" Rodriguez	second base	right	right	.304
Kid Rabbit Winkle	substitute third base	right	right	.299
Gasser Phipps	center field	right	right	.305[**]
Lou "Skip-to-My-Lou" Clementine	manager			

[*]Average with the Orange Park Alligators of the Greater Jacksonville, Florida, Citrus League
[**]Injured

Score for the season opener:

Team	1	2	3	4	5	6	R	H	E
HCH	2	0	1	0	0	0	3	7	2
RAM	1	0	0	0	4	X	5	5	0

W: Slingshot Slocum, L: Dirty Joe Dartoe

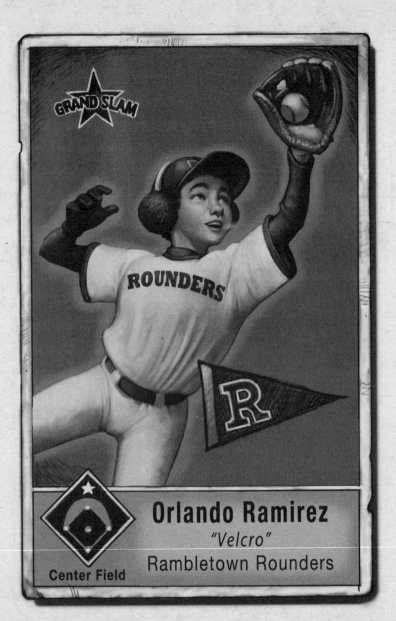

GRAND SLAM

ROUNDERS

R

Orlando Ramirez
"Velcro"
Rambletown Rounders

Center Field

A Q&A with the Author: Kevin Markey on Wacky
Writing, Wacky Weather, and Wacky Baseball

Kevin Markey's Top-Ten
Favorite Baseball Books of All Time

A Sneak Peek at the Next Book in the
Super Sluggers Series, *Wing Ding*

A Q&A with the Author: Kevin Markey on Wacky Writing, Wacky Weather, and Wacky Baseball

Where do you get your ideas for the wacky weather in the Super Sluggers books?

More than any other major sport, baseball is at the mercy of the weather. Indoor sports like basketball and hockey obviously can be played no matter what's happening outside. Football and soccer are rarely cancelled because of lousy conditions. The field turns into a bog (or a frozen tundra) and the action gets slow and sloppy, but it's still possible to move the ball forward. Baseball isn't like that. It really can't be played in bad weather. If the ball gets slippery, pitchers can't throw it and hitters can't hit it.

Because baseball is so closely tied to weather (Is there anything sadder than the ump calling a game?), crazy plagues of atmospheric oddities make a natural subject for the Super Sluggers. *Slumpbuster* was inspired in part by classic baseball photographs. The players in their sweltering flannel uniforms always look so gritty and hot. A blistering heat wave and drought set the right tone for the book. *Wall Ball* is more about the frustration of waiting for something you really, really want. In Massachusetts, where I live, winters are cold and long and often very snowy. Everybody looks forward to spring with growing excitement, and just when we think the thaw has finally arrived, we always seem to get a late-season snow fall that sets us back a few more days. I think everybody can relate to waiting for spring. Especially baseball fans!

In *Wing Ding*, the weather once again turns against the

Rounders. A massive windstorm blows a huge swarm of grass-hoppers into Rambletown. Guess what grasshoppers eat. That's right—grass. As Walloper says, "You can't play base-ball if grasshoppers have devoured the field." Not to mention gale-force wind makes the ball do crazy things.

What's the strangest weather-related event in baseball history?
Probably the most famous example of natural forces affecting a baseball game happened during the 1989 World Series between the San Francisco Giants and the Oakland Athlet-ics. Billed as the Battle of the Bay because the two California cities sit right across San Francisco Bay from each other, the series came to a screeching halt on October 17, when the Loma Prieta earthquake struck during warm-ups for Game 3. The TV broadcast had already begun and viewers all across the country actually saw Oakland-Alameda County Coliseum, home to the A's, shaking for a couple seconds before the pic-ture broke up.

Measuring almost 7 on the Richter scale, the quake was the largest to occur on the San Andreas Fault since the famous San Francisco Earthquake of 1906. Although the Loma Prieta quake lasted only 10 to 15 seconds, Game 3 was cancelled instantly, and the series was suspended for ten days. When play resumed, the Athletics completed a four-game sweep of the Giants.

Do you think baseball inspires hilarity?
Definitely, if only because there have always been so many colorful and obsessively superstitious characters who've played the game. Guys like Hall of Fame third baseman Wade Boggs, who always ate a chicken dinner before games. He thought it

made him hit better. Who knows, maybe he was right. Boggs led the American League five times in batting.

Then there was manager George Stallings of the old Boston Braves, who was so superstitious he would freeze in the middle of whatever he was doing whenever one of his players got a hit. One time he happened to be bending down to pick up a peanut shell from the dugout floor when the batter smacked the ball. Stallings held his pose. The Braves proceeded to rally, knocking ten straight hits. By the time the marathon inning finally ended, poor old Stallings was all knotted up with muscle spasms. His players had to carry him out of the dugout.

What are some of your favorite funny quotes by baseball players/ coaches/fans?

Yankee legend Yogi Berra is an endless font of funny sayings, known for such classic lines as "Ninety percent of this game is half mental" and "Nobody goes there anymore. It's too crowded." Yogi claims he got credit for more funny comments than he really deserved. His exact words were, "I really didn't say everything I said." (Makes sense, I guess.)

My other great baseball quotes include:

"There's one word that tells you everything about baseball: You never know."—Pitcher Joaquin Andujar

"Good pitching will beat good hitting anytime, and vice versa." —Pitcher Bob Veale

"I made a game effort to argue, but two things were against me: the umpire and the rules." —Manager Leo Durocher

"There are two theories on hitting the knuckleball. Unfortunately, neither of them work."

—Legendary hitting coach Charlie Lau

"My pitching philosophy is simple. Keep the ball away from the bat."—Pitcher Satchel Paige

"The doctors X-rayed my head and found nothing."

—Pitcher Dizzy Dean

"Trying to throw a fastball by Hank Aaron is like trying to sneak a sunrise past a rooster." —Pitcher Curt Simmons

"Sandy's fastball was so fast, some batters would start to swing as he was on his way to the mound."

—Sportswriter Jim Murray, on Hall of Fame pitcher Sandy Koufax

"When you're in a slump, it's almost as if you look out at the field and it's one big glove." —Third baseman Vance Law

"Why does everybody stand up and sing 'Take Me Out to the Ballgame' when they're already there?"

—Actor Larry Anderson

"The trouble with baseball is that it is not played the year round."—Pitcher Gaylord Perry

Kevin Markey's Top-Ten Favorite Baseball Books of All Time

Baseball seems to inspire writers more than any other sport. Part of the reason for this, I think, is that the action unfolds with the natural rhythm of a good story, each inning becoming its own chapter in the book of a game. As a result, you could fill a whole library with nothing but baseball stories.

In alphabetical order, here are ten of my favorites—a book for each inning, plus a bonus: this game is so close it definitely needs at least one extra inning!

ABNER AND ME and the rest of the Baseball Card Adventure series by Dan Gutman
I love how Dan Gutman uses baseball to write about some of the most interesting and intense moments in American history. He chooses great subjects and packs his stories with action and excitement.

THE BASEBALL ENCYCLOPEDIA
In my opinion, the best sports reference book bar none. Numbering more than 3,000 pages, the massive volume contains the complete stats of *every* single major league ballplayer *ever* to play the game. When I first encountered it as a teenager, I was blown away by all the information. I still am. The only problem is that it hasn't been updated since 1996.

THE GLORY OF THEIR TIMES: *The Story of the Early Days of Baseball Told by the Men Who Played It* by Lawrence S. Ritter
Many years ago author Lawrence Ritter traveled around the country seeking out and interviewing a Hall of Fame roster of

legendary players—Babe Ruth, Smoky Joe Wood, and Goose Goslin, among others. He preserved their memories in this priceless book. By turns heroic, comical, and tragic, the collection is always entertaining. You can find it in the adult section of the bookstore.

THE KID FROM TOMKINSVILLE by John R. Tunis
A classic from one of the greatest authors ever. Forget that the novel was written before Jumbotrons, artificial turf, or aluminum bats were invented. The story of Roy "the Kid" Tucker, a big-league rookie in need of seasoning, sizzles with action and timeless baseball wisdom.

MANIAC MAGEE by Jerry Spinelli
This funny and moving novel tells the wild adventures of Jeffrey "Maniac" Magee, an eleven-year-old orphan who runs away from his mean aunt and uncle to find his own way in life. Though not strictly a baseball novel, there's a lot of baseball in it. (One of my favorite parts is when Maniac smashes a homer off a big bully who happens to be the best pitcher in town.)

ONCE MORE AROUND THE PARK: *A Baseball Reader* by Roger Angell
Also in the adult section, another collection of articles by one of our very finest baseball writers. Make that writers, any subject. Reading Roger Angell is like sharing box seats with the world's most insightful and appreciative fan. Bonus fact: Mr. Angell's stepfather was E. B. White, the man who wrote CHARLOTTE'S WEB and STUART LITTLE. Quite a family!

SUMMERLAND by Michael Chabon

A magical fable about an unlikely boy-hero named Ethan Feld, who is spirited away to a mystical world of giants, werefoxes, screaming demons, and gentle Sasquatches to save the universe through baseball. Michael Chabon's imagination knows no bounds and his tale, drawing on Native American folklore and classical mythology, delivers heart-thumping excitement from the very first pitch.

The Super Sluggers series by Kevin Markey

What can I say? It's my list and I get to choose what goes on it. Besides, it's true: The Super Sluggers stories are among my favorites. Not only are they playful and exciting (if I may say so myself), they're also a world of fun to write.

THE ULTIMATE BASEBALL BOOK, edited by Dan Okrent and Harris Lewine

Let's see . . . a blow-by-blow account of every major league season since the first one way back in 1876? Check. Tons of amazing photographs spanning the full history of the game? Check. Essays by some of the best sportswriters in the business? Check again. Oh yes, one last reason I love this book: Fresh out of college, I got to write captions for it. Maybe the coolest job I've ever had.

WE ARE THE SHIP: *The Story of Negro League Baseball* by Kadir Nelson

Kadir Nelson sets his colorful account of the great Negro League teams and their stars (Satchel Paige, Cool Papa Bell, Josh Gibson) during the league's barnstorming heyday, and he graces the action with his stunningly beautiful paintings. Simply mesmerizing.

9

Tugboat Tooley spotted it first.

Tugboat plays catcher for the Rambletown Rounders baseball team, reigning champs of the ten-to-twelve division.

I play third base.

My name is the Great Walloper, Walloper for short. At least that's what everybody calls me, because I like to wallop the tar out of the ball. My real name, the one my parents gave me, is Banjo. Banjo H. Bishbash, to be precise. The *H* stands for Hit. People ask me about my name all the time. "So unusual," they say.

It gets tiring.

For the record, Hit was my mom's last name before she married my dad. Banjo is my grand-father's name and my dad's, too. Like the musical instrument. For real.

You can see why I prefer Walloper.

At the moment I wasn't worried about any of that. I was more concerned with keeping the St. Joe Jungle Cats from tying the score.

It was the top of the third inning, no outs, a fair breeze blowing straight in from center. Our pitcher, Slingshot Slocum, stood on the mound protecting a slim 2–1 lead. A St. Joe runner bounced on his toes at second base. From the way he kept glancing in my direction, I knew he was thinking about stealing third.

Crouched behind home plate, Tugboat surveyed the diamond. Nothing gets past Tugboat. Not balls, not base runners, not even the hot-dog man out in the bleachers making change for a five spot. Tugboat's our field general and we rely on him.

A real general would have been nice. He would've had an army at his command. As we were about to learn, we could've used an army. Maybe the air force, too. Send in the marines just to be safe.

Tugboat flashed a sign. One finger. That meant fastball. A fastball is not a good pitch to steal on.

It gets to the plate too quickly. If Slingshot blazed the ball home and Tugboat made a good peg to me, we'd have a good shot at cutting down the runner. All I had to do was make a clean catch and apply the tag.

I shot a look toward second. I wondered if the runner could see Tugboat's signals as clearly as I could. I hoped not.

At the plate, the St. Joe hitter, batting lefty, dug into the box. He zeroed in on Slingshot like a laser beam. The umpire hunkered down behind Tugboat, one hand resting lightly on the catcher's right shoulder for balance. The ump, too, was completely focused on Slingshot.

Slingshot kicked and fired a fastball. The St. Joe batter started his swing.

That's when Tugboat sprang from behind the plate.

"Time out!" he called, flinging away his mask.

He bounced up so quickly, I thought a bee had stung him.

Tugboat's sudden leap knocked the ump

backward, toppling him onto his backside behind home plate. I don't know what the ump thought. Probably how much he was going to enjoy tossing Tugboat out of the game. While all this was happening, the batter lunged at the pitch and sent the ball dribbling toward short.

"You can't call time in the middle of a pitch!" the ump barked from the dirt.

Tugboat didn't say a word. As the hitter took off for first, he just pointed to center field. We whipped our heads around to see what was bothering him. All except Stump Plumwhiff, our shortstop, that is. As I turned, I saw Stump charge the slow roller coming his way and rush a throw to our first baseman, Gilly Wishes.

Then I looked to the outfield to see what had caused Tugboat to act so strangely.

What I witnessed made my knees quake.

A huge, shimmering cloud filled the sky. Shaped sort of like an ice-cream cone lying on its side, it stretched all the way to the horizon. Whatever it was, it was moving.

Fast.

Straight toward us.

The leading edge, where the cone came to a point, dived straight over the high wooden out-field fence. A second later a terrible noise filled my ears. The sound grew louder and louder as the spiraling black thing swirled closer and closer. It buzzed like a million vacuum cleaners sucking up everything in their path.

"What in the world is that?" I shouted.

"It's an error," Stump said dejectedly as his throw sailed over Gilly's head and into the grandstand.

Stump and I always talk out on the diamond. Usually we stick to baseball chatter. "Two, four, six, eight, our pitcher's looking great!" Stuff like that. "Batter, batter, what's the matter? Swing, batter!"

"Forget the throw," I said, pointing toward the outfield. "What is that thing?"

Stump looked up and finally caught his first glimpse of the buzzing cone. His eyes were only a little bigger than stop signs as he said, "Walloper, I do believe it's a tornado!"

"I never saw a tornado that moved sideways," I shouted back over the rising din.

In fact I had never seen a tornado at all except in movies. This didn't look like any Hollywood twister.

We call Stump "Stump" because he has an answer for everything. You can never stump him. If he doesn't know the answer, he makes one up. If Stump said this thing was a tornado, I was prepared to believe him.

"Run for your lives!" I shouted.

My teammates were way ahead of me.

Literally.

Most of them were already halfway to our low concrete dugout on the third-base side of the diamond. The St. Joe base runners chugged past us going the other way. They didn't bother to stay inside the base paths. It looked more like a footrace than a baseball game.

Just then a remote-control helicopter fell out of the sky. It landed with a whine, smack in the middle of the diamond.

Another one plunged to the ground behind it.

Then another and another.

An armor-plated green one swooped down and knocked Stump's cap off his head as he scrambled for cover. One thing you should know about Stump: he practically never takes off his cap. He wears it summer and winter, day and night. He probably wears it in the shower. The sight of his stand-up red hair was shocking.

But not nearly as shocking as what was dropping onto the field.

It wasn't helicopters at all. It was grasshoppers. Millions and millions of huge grasshoppers.

My first reaction was relief. That massive black cloud wasn't a tornado after all. My second was a severe case of the heebie-jeebies: bugs covered every inch of the field. More poured over the fence every second. In the stands, screaming fans climbed all over one another to reach the exits.

The umpire waved his hands in the air.

"I'm calling the game," he said. "It's canceled due to grasshoppers."

Then he kicked up his heels and joined the

mass exodus from Rambletown Field. Within a few minutes, the ballpark was completely deserted. Deserted by fans, that is. The insect population had never been higher.

From the safety of the dugout, my teammates and I watched the cloud of bugs settle on the field. It was like having a front-row ticket to one of those nature programs on the Animal Channel on TV: "When Grasshoppers Attack!"

Except that it was real.

And it was live.

And instead of in some far-off savanna in Africa or wherever, it was happening right here in Rambletown.